THE WESTERN FRONTIER LIBRARY
(*Complete list on pages 319–22*)

STEPSONS OF LIGHT

Stepsons of Light

by
Eugene Manlove Rhodes

with an Introduction by
W. H. Hutchinson

and

Illustrations by
W. H. D. Koerner

NORMAN
UNIVERSITY OF OKLAHOMA PRESS

Library of Congress Catalog Card Number: 69–16714

Copyright 1920 by The Curtis Publishing Company, 1921 by Hough-
ton Mifflin Company, and 1949 by Rhodes estate. New edition copyright 1969 by the University of Oklahoma Press, Publishing Division
of the University. Manufactured in the U.S.A. First printing of the
new edition.

2186405

To my wife

—E. M. R.

INTRODUCTION

By W. H. Hutchinson

THERE are those today who sense O. Henry's influence in Rhodes's writings, and this may be reflected hereinafter by the unsolved question of the three bullets that made a corpse of Caney when Charlie See had fired but twice. Disputes among true Rhodesians on this point have been known to reach unseemly proportions. Be this O. Henryesque or not, the fact remains that Eugene Manlove Rhodes never claimed more for himself than the accolade awarded Robert Louis Stevenson, "Teller of Tales."

Fidelity to time and place and incident, fidelity to his land and its people and their values—this fidelity was Rhodes's hallmark. It is stamped deeply into the pages of *Stepsons of Light*, which here is reprinted for the first time since World War II, when the Council of Books in Wartime distributed almost 100,000 copies to members of the armed services.

STEPSONS OF LIGHT

The gold discovery which carries the plot mechanism is laid in fiction where it occurred in fact: in the Caballo Mountains on the east side of the Río Grande above the hamlet of Garfield, New Mexico. Dry-washing placers were discovered there in 1901 by Encarnación Silva, who kept his find to himself until November, 1903, when he got *muy borracho* in Hillsboro and let it leak away. Rhodes's skillful interweaving of this fact with the lost-mine legends of the land he loved prompted J. Frank Dobie to use a long excerpt from *Stepsons* in his classic *Apache Gold and Yaqui Silver* (1939).

The description in *Stepsons* of the Bar Cross horse camp is a photographic description of Rhodes's own ranch in the San Andrés Mountains, which he leased upon straitened occasion to the Bar Cross, more formally known as the Detroit & Rio Grande Livestock Company. The methodology of the Bar Cross roundup is archaelogically accurate, down to the names of the riders with the wagon. The tale's account of the Bar Cross cook's building dinner for forty men in twenty minutes is related as fact by N. Howard "Jack" Thorp in his *Pardner of the Wind* (1945). The tale's "George Scarboro" was in life the veritable George

INTRODUCTION

Scarborough, a most notable *pistolero* who killed John Selman, the slayer of John Wesley "Forty Notches" Hardin, and was himself erased by Will Carver of the Wild Bunch.

Yet another Rhodesian hallmark is plainly seen hereafter: his portrayal of the distaff side of a love story, a process best compared to that employed by a skittish bronc crossing boggy ground. Bernard DeVoto once observed that Rhodes's maidens were "infrangibly virginal," and Rhodes himself made wry comment that Sir Walter Scott had almost ruined him. Nonetheless, Rhodes's idealized heroines reflect truly the life he had known firsthand: there were in general but two kinds of women—good and bad—in the West-That-Was. Or as William Barclay "Bat" Masterson is said to have said to this writer's father, "My wife was the only *woman* in Dodge; all the rest were *ladies*," meaning companions for revenue only. Rhodes had known both kinds; he chose to write about the best of the good. In so doing, he made them what Miss May Bailey had been to him in his ardent youth—an ennobling inspiration to a masculine society in a raw, harsh land. Even so would Rhodes have preferred the honest prostitutes of his time to today's amateur cult of indiscriminate coupling, if for no other reason than that an honest whore did not pretend to be what she was not.

With the hallmarks noted, it is seemly to call attention to the most unusual aspect of this or any other Rhodesian tale. It encompasses some ten pages and makes an essayish jeremiad against the literary "realists" of the period and against their "realism," which Rhodes once quite wickedly dubbed "the Conrad Aiken–void."

This passage makes an abrupt fault on the vein of Rhodes's story. Perhaps no magazine of the 1920's except the *Saturday Evening Post* would have accepted Rhodes's tale with this distraction in it. It is doubtful, too, whether the *Post* would have allowed any other of its authors to get away with such a complaint. Why it did may be explained in part by an opinion voiced by Mody C. Boatright in the *Southwest Review* (Summer, 1951) during a discussion of Owen Wister: "George Horace Lorimer, who took over the editorship of the *Saturday Evening Post* in 1898, and frankly made it the voice of American Business, assembled a stable of western writers . . . including Owen Wister, and through them kept before his readers the cowboy as a symbol of the rugged individualism that had made America great."

INTRODUCTION

Inasmuch as the then current literary luminaries were as one in disparaging America—the babbitt-warren—Rhodes's intrusive essay was in keeping with this editorial policy. With due respect to Mody Boatright, however, it should be noted here, and right firmly, that Rhodes was no ory-eyed partisan of the Establishment that, in Boatright's view, Lorimer and his magazine served well. It also should be noted with equal firmness that Rhodes had nothing in common with the pioneers' descendants who inhabited Gopher Prairie or Sauk Center or Middletown or Winesburg.

In this essay, Rhodes voiced his resolute rejection of the views about his country and its people that made the stock in trade of H. L. Mencken, George Jean Nathan, Ludwig Lewisohn, Waldo Frank, and Sherwood Anderson. To this group he added Van Wyck Brooks for his treatment of Mark Twain and F. Scott Fitzgerald for cause. These writers constituted the self-styled "Civilized Minority" in American letters, the "Young Intellectuals" of the "Revolting School." At the risk of making a chauvinist out of a frontiersman, Rhodes found them revolting, true enough, but little more.

Rhodes had been molded on and by the frontier

for thirty-seven years before spending the ensuing twenty-eight as a novelist of that experience. He had the deep-seated mistrust of the man who had worked with his hands between a rock and a hard place for those who rode a literary sidesaddle and proclaimed their mission to be that of saviors of the working class. Rhodes clearly sensed that behind their semantical façade of uplifting the downtrodden lay the arrogant belief that the downtrodden would be infinitely improved by a state of permanent subordination to the saviors' plans for their salvation. Like the best of frontiersmen since our westering began, Rhodes believed that any and every elite group should be opposed with all the ardency that could be mustered. He continued his opposition in print, wherever and whenever opportunity afforded, until he died.

Rhodes had learned virtually at birth that his land and its people, the post–Civil War agricultural and pastoral frontiers, were the exploited provinces of the financial and political East. His almost anarchical attitude toward exploiters in these fields gained vehemence, even a shrillness lacking in his other writings, when he directed it against the literati who admired the city in fulsome cadences while despising all else as the abode of

INTRODUCTION

Rose Benét, the later founders of the *Saturday Review of Literature*: "This is a propaganda novel of the National Security League school. The author has little use for the dissenter, the realist, or the English language."

Rhodes's reaction to such superciliousness already had been made, and he would have the same reaction to today's even more sourly nihilistic evaluations of past and present American strivings and values: "Have we toiled for twice twenty centuries to be rid of impudent priests, arrogant aristocrats, and imbecile kings, only to be pestered now by sophomores?" To this he might have added another phrase of his own coinage, "If this be reason, make the most of it"!

Chico State College
Chico, California

ILLUSTRATIONS

The paintings made by W. H. D. Koerner for *Stepsons of Light* are printed here by permission of Mrs. Ruth Koerner Oliver.

STEPSONS OF LIGHT

STEPSONS OF LIGHT

T HERE are two sorts of people—those who point with pride and those who view with alarm. They are quite right. The world will not soon forget Parkman "of Ours." Here was a man of learning, common sense, judgment and wide sympathies. Yet once he stumbled; the paregorical imperative, which impels each of us to utter ignominious nonsense, urged Francis Parkman to the like unhappiness, drove him to father and put forth this void and singular statement:

I have often perplexed myself to divine the various motives that give impulse to this strange migration; but whatever they may be, whether an insane hope of a better condition of life, or a desire of shaking off the restraints of law and society, or mere restlessness, certain it is that multitudes bitterly repent the journey.

The year was 1846; the place, Independence, in Missouri; that strange migration was

the winning of the West. Mr. Parkman
viewed it with alarm. The passage quoted
may yet be found in the first chapter of "The
Oregon Trail." We, wise after the event,
now point with pride to that strange migration
of our fathers. The Great Trek has lasted
three hundred years. To-day we dimly perceive that the history of America is the story
of the pioneer; that on our shifting frontiers
the race has been hammered and tempered to
a cutting edge.

That insane hope of better things—the same
which beckoned on the Israelites and the Pil-
grim Fathers; restraints of law and society,
which in Egypt made the Israelite a slave, in
England gave the Puritan to the pillory and
the stocks, and in this western world of ours
took the form of a hollow squire, founder by
letters patent of a landed oligarchy—so that
the bold and venturesome sought homes in the
unsquired wilderness; and restlessness, that
quality which marks the most notable difference between man and sandstone. Restlessness, shaking off restraints, insane hopes—in
that cadence of ideas what is there of haunt-

ing, echolike and familiar? Restraints of society? When the very stones of the streets shrieked at him the name of that town—Independence! Now we know the words that haunted us: "Life, liberty, and the pursuit of happiness!" Never was echo clearer. The emigrants were there in exercise of those unavoidable rights. Not happiness, or the overtaking of happiness; the pursuit of happiness —the insane hope of a better condition of life.

That which perplexed Parkman looked upon, disapproving, was the settlement of America—the greatest upbuilding of recorded time; and the prime motive of that great migration was the motive of all migrations— the search for food and land. They went west for food. What they did there was to work; if you require a monument—take a good look!

Here is the record of a few late camp fires of the Great Trek.

I

"Why-Why had been principally beaten about the face, and his injuries, therefore, were slight."
—*The Romance of the First Radical.*

"A fine face, marred by an expression of unscrupulous integrity."   —*Credit Lost.*

THE lady listened with fluttering attention. The lady was sweet and twenty, and the narrator—myself—was spurred to greater effort. Suddenly a thought struck her. It was a severe blow. She sat up straight, she stiffened her lips to primness, her fine eyes darkened with suspicion, her voice crisped to stern inquiry.

"I suppose, when Sunday came, you kept right on working?"

It was an acid supposition. Her dear little nose squinched to express some strong emotion —loving-kindness, perhaps; her dear little upper lip curled ominous. She looked as though she might bite.

"Kept right on working is right. We had to keep on working," I explained. "We couldn't very well work six days gathering

12

cattle and then turn them all loose again on the seventh day—could we now?"

The lady frowned. The lady sniffed. She was not one to be turned aside by subterfuge. She leaned forward to strike, and flattened her brows in scorn. She looked uncommonly like a rattlesnake. She said:

"I suppose you couldn't put them in the barn-yards?"

And I learned about readers from her.

Cattle were once grazed to the nearest rail-road—say, a thousand miles—yes, and beyond that railroad to Wyoming grass; or Montana. No one who saw those great herds forgot them or ever quite refrained from speech of those stirring days, to children or grandchildren. That is why so many think—not unnaturally —that range cattle were always held under herd. But it is a mistaken impression. Cattle do not thrive under herd.

Cattle on the free range—everybody's cattle—were turned loose and mixed together. There were no fences except as deep rivers counted for such; the Panama Canal was yet

undug.   Twice a year, in spring and fall,
everybody gets together to work the cattle at
the rodeo, or round-up.   They brand the
calves; they take into the day herd all strays,
all steers or cows to be shipped, and nothing
more.   From cattle gathered each day steers
and strays are cut out and thrown into the day
herd; all the others, the range cattle, are turned loose with a vigorous shove in that direction most remote from to-morrow's round-up.

Again, your ranch was that land to which
you had either title or claim; its purpose was
to give a water right on stream or lake or to
hold spring, well or tank.   But your range
was either Texas land or Uncle Sam's land
as far as your cattle would range from your
various water rights—say, twenty-five miles in
each direction.   Your range was that country
where you were reasonably sure your cattle
would not be stolen by strangers.

Here was the way of the Bar Cross
round-up; with slight variations it was the
way of any round-up.   The Bar Cross Company, running the biggest brand on the Jornada range, supplied one foreman, one straw

boss, three top hands and the captain of the day herd; one horse wrangler, who herded the saddle horses by day; one night wrangler, who herded them by night; and mounts for these eight. The Bar Cross also furnished one red-headed cook; one chuck wagon and the chuck—chuck being grub—and one bed wagon to haul bed rolls from camp to camp, and also to haul wood and water between times. Item: Four mules for the chuck wagon, and two for the bed wagon. The night wrangler drove the bed wagon; night wranglers were not supposed to sleep.

Other ranchmen, co-users of the Bar Cross range, sent each a man and his mount to represent. A man with many cattle might send two or more men; the 7 T X—next to the Bar Cross the biggest brand on the Jornada—sent four. Each man or each two men brought tarp and bedding on a pack horse.

From north, south, east and west came the stray men, each with mount and bed. Stray men stayed with the outfit as long as it pleased them. When they were satisfied they cut out from the day herd their own cattle, together

with those of their neighbors, and drove them
home.   As a usual thing, three or four would
throw in and drive back together. If by
chance some man was homeward bound and
alone, the Bar Cross detailed a man to help
him home; a friendly and not imprudent
custom.

To sum up: The Bar Cross paid nine men,
and provided good grub for all comers; in
return it had the help of twenty-five to forty
men in working the range; the rodeo, or
round-up.

During the weeks or months of that working, wherever some other outfit gave a
round-up—east, west, south or north—there,
with mount and bed, went either a Bar Cross
man or one from some other brand of the
Jornada people, bringing back all Jornada
cattle.

A word about horses.   In the fall, when
grass was green and good, a mount was eight
to thirteen head.   One must be gentle; he was
night horse; every man stood guard at night
two and a half to three hours; all night in
case of storm.   For the others, the best were

cutting horses, used afternoons, when the day's drive was worked; the poorest were circle horses and were ridden in the forenoon, when the round-up was made. But in the spring it is different. Grass is scant and short; corn is fed, and four horses go to a mount; the range is worked lightly.

So much was needful by way of glossary and guide; so partly to avoid such handicap as we meet in telling a baseball story to an Englishman.

It is a singular thing that with the Bar Cross were found the top ropers, crack riders, sure shots—not only the slickest cowmen, but also the wisest cow ponies. Our foremen were "cowmen right," our wranglers held the horses, our cooks would fry anything once. But you know how it is—your own organization—firm, farm or factory—is doubtless the best of its kind. No? You surprise me. You have missed much—faith in others, hope for others, comradeship.

It is laughable to recall that men of other brands disputed the headship of the Bar Cross. Nor was this jest or bravado; the poor fellows

were sincere enough.   Indeed, we thought this
pathetic loyalty rather admirable than otherwise.   Such were the 101, in Colorado; the
X I T, in the Panhandle; the Block and the
V V, between the Pecos and the Front Range;
the Bar W, west of the White Mountain; the
V Cross T, the John Cross, the Diamond A
and the L C, west of the Rio Grande.   Even
from Arizona, the T L, the Toltec Company
—Little Colorado River way—put forth absurd pretensions.

The Bar Cross men smiled, knowing what
they knew.   That sure knowledge was the
foundation of the gay and holdfast spirit they
brought to confront importunate life.   No
man wanted to be the weak link of that strong
chain; each brought to his meanest task the
earnestness that is remarked upon when Mr.
Ty Cobb slides into second base; they bent
every energy on the thing they did at the joyful time of doing it.   In this way only is developed that rare quality to which the scientific give the name of pep or punch.   Being
snappy made them happy, and being happy
made them snappy; establishing what is

known to philosophers as the virtuous circle. The nearest parallel is newspaper circulation, which means more advertising, which boosts circulation, and so onward and upward.

In that high eagerness of absorption, a man "working for the brand" did not, could not, center all thoughts on self; he trusted his fellows, counted upon them, joyed in their deeds. And to forget self in the thought of others is for so long to reach life at its highest.

The Bar Cross had worked the northern half of the range, getting back to Engle, the center and the one shipping point of the Jornada, with fifteen hundred steers—finding there no cars available, no prospect of cars for ten days to come. To take those steers to the south and back meant that they would be so gaunted as to be unfit for shipment.

So the wagon led on softly, drifting down to the river, to a beating of bosques for outlaw cattle and a combing of half-forgotten ridges and pockets behind Christobal Mountain. It was a work which because of its difficulty had been shirked for years; the river cattle mostly came out on the plains in the rainy season, and got their just deserts there. Waiting for cars, the outfit was marking time anyhow.   Any cattle snared on the river were pure gain.   The main point was to handle the stock tenderly.   From working the bosques the outfit expected few cattle and got less.— The poets babble about the bosky dell; bosque, literally translated, means "woods."   Yet for this purpose if you understand the word as "jungle," you will be the less misled.

Johnny Dines sat tailor-wise on his horse at the crest of a sandy knoll and looked down at the day herd, spread out over a square mile of tableland, and now mostly asleep in the brooding heat of afternoon.   About the herd other riders, six in all, stood at attention, black silhouettes, or paced softly to turn back would-be stragglers.

Of these riders Neighbor Jones alone was a Bar Cross man.   He was captain of the day herd, a fixture; for him reluctant straymen were detailed in turn, day by day, as day herders.   Johnny represented a number of small brands in the north end of the Black Range.

His face was sparkling, all alive; he was short, slender, black-haired, black-eyed, two and twenty. He saw—Neighbor Jones himself not sooner—what turmoil rose startling from a lower bench to riverward; a riot of wild cattle with riders as wild on lead and swing and point. As a usual thing, the day's catch comes sedately to the day herd; but this day's catch was bosque cattle—renegades and desperates of a dozen brands.

Jody Weir, on Johnny's right, sat on the sand in the shadow of his horses. This was not ethical; seeing him, Yoast and Ralston, leading the riot, turned that way, drew aside to right and left, and so loosed the charging hurricane directly at the culprit.

Weir scrambled to saddle and spurred from under. The other riders closed in on the day herd, stirring them up the better to check the outlaws. Half of the round-up crew followed Yoast to the right of the now roused and bellowing day herd, bunching them; the others followed Ralston on Johnny's side of the herd.

Cole Ralston was the Bar Cross foreman. Overtaking Johnny, he raised a finger; the two drew rein and let the others pass by. Cole spoke to the last man.

"Spike, when they quiet down you ride round and tell all these day-herder waddies that if any of 'em want to write letters they can slip in to the wagon. I'm sending a man to town soon after supper."

He turned to Johnny, laughing.

"Them outcasts was sure snaky. We near wasted the whole bunch. Had to string 'em out and let 'em run so they thought they was getting away or they'd ha' broke back into the brush."

"Two bull fights started already," observed Johnny. "Your Sunday-School bulls are hunting up the wild ones, just a-snuffin'."

"The boys will keep 'em a-moving," said Cole. "Dines, you ride your own horses, so I reckon you're not drawing pay from the ninety-seven piney-woods brands you're lookin' out for. Just turning their cattle in a neighborly way?"

"Someone had to come."

"Well, then," said Cole, "how would you like a Bar Cross mount?"

Slow red tinged the olive of Johnny's cheek, betraying the quickened heartbeats.

"You've done hired a hand—quick as ever I throw these cattle back home."

"Wouldn't Walter Hearn cut out your milk-pen brands as close as you would?"

"Sure! He's one of the bunch."

"Your pay started this morning, then. Here's the lay. To-morrow we work the herd and start the west-bound strays home. Walt can throw in with the S S Bar man and I'll send Lon along to represent the Bar Cross. Hiram goes to the John Cross work, at the same time helpin' Pink throw back the John Cross stuff. So that leaves us shy a short man. That's you. Send your horses home with Walt."

"I'd like to keep one with me for my private."

"All right. Leave him at the horse camp. Can't carry any idlers with the *caballada*—makes the other horses discontented. You drift into the wagon early, when you see the horse herd coming. I'm goin' to send you to the horse camp to get you a mount. We'll cut out all the lame ones and sore backs from our mounts too. I'll give you a list of fresh ones to bring back for us. You go up to Engle after supper and then slip out to Moongate to-morrow. We'll be loadin' 'em at Engle when you get back. No hurry; take your time."

He rode on. Behind him the most joyous heart between two oceans thumped at Johnny's ribs. It is likely that you see no cause for pride. You see a hard job for a scanty wage; to Johnny Dines it was accolade and shoulder stroke. Johnny's life so far had been made up all of hardships well borne. But that was what Johnny did not know or dream; to-day, hailed man-grown, he thought of his honors, prince and peer, not as deserved and earned, but as an unmerited stroke of good fortune.

The herd, suddenly roused, became vociferous with query and rumor; drifted uneasily a little, muttered, whispered, tittered, fell quiet again, to cheerful grazing. The fresh wild cattle, nearing the periphery, glimpsed the dreaded horsemen beyond, and turned again to hiding in the center.   Cole and most of his riders drew away and paced soberly camp-ward, leaving ten herders where they found six.

Jody Weir rode over to Johnny.

"Old citizen," he said, "the rod tells me you are for Engle, and if I wanted to send letters I might go write 'em.   But I beat him to it. Letter to my girl all written and ready.   All I had to do was to put in a line with my little old pencil, telling her we'd work the herd to-morrow and start home next day.   She'll be one pleased girl; she sure does love her little Jody."

Johnny knotted his brows in puzzlement. "But who reads your letters to her?" he said wonderingly.

"Now what you doin'—tryin' to slur my girl?   She's educated, that child is."

"No; but when you said she—she liked her little Jody—why, I naturally supposed"— Johnny hesitated—"her eyesight, you know, might be—"

Weir slapped his leg and guffawed.

"Thought she was blind, did you? Well, she ain't. If she was I wouldn't be writing this letter. Most of it is heap private and confidential." His face took on a broad and knowing leer as he handed over the letter. It was fat; it was face up; it bore the address:

MR. J. D. WEIR, HILLSBORO, N. M.

Johnny put the letter carefully in his saddle pocket.

"Don't you think maybe you're leaving an opening for some of the cattle to slip out?" he said, twitching his thumb toward Weir's deserted post.

"Let them other waddies circulate a little— lazy dogs! Won't hurt 'em any. Cattle ain't troublin', nohow. Cole, he told me himself to slide over and give you my letters. Darned funny if a man can't gas a little once in a while." He gave Johnny a black look. "Say, feller! Maybe you don't like my talk?"

"No," said Johnny, "I don't. Not unless you change the subject. That young lady wouldn't want you to be talking her over with any tough you meet."

Jody Weir checked his horse and regarded Dines with a truculent stare. "Aw, hell! She ain't so particular! Here, let me show you the stuff she writes, herself." His hand went to his vest pocket. "Some baby!"

"Here! That's enough! I'm surprised at you, Jody. I never was plumb foolish about you, but I suhtenly thought you was man enough not to kiss and tell. That's as low-down as they ever get, I reckon."

"You ain't got no gun. And you're too little for me to maul round—say nothing of scaring the herd and maybe wasting a lot."

"All that is very true—to-day. But it isn't a question of guns, just now. I'm trying to get you to shut up that big blackguard mouth of yours. If you wasn't such a numskull you'd see that I'm a-doin' you a good turn."

"You little sawed-off, bench-legged pup! I orter throw this gun away and stomp you into the sand! Aw, what's a-bitin' you? I ain't named no names, have I? You're crowdin' me purty hard. What's the matter, feller? Got it in for me, and usin' this as an excuse? When'd I ever do you any dirt?"

"Never," said Johnny. "Get this straight: I'm not wanting any fight. It's decency I'm trying to crowd on to you—not a fight."

"I can't write to my girl without your say-so, hey?"

"Now you listen! Writing to a girl, fair and above-board, is one thing. Writing unbeknownst to her folks, with loose talk about her on the side, is another thing altogether. It's yourself you're doing dirt to—and to this girl that trusted you."

Jody's face showed real bewilderment. "How? You don't know her name. Nobody knows her name. No one knows I have more than a nodding acquaintance with her—unless she told you!" His eyes flamed with sudden suspicion. "You know her yourself—she told you!"

"Jody, you put me in mind of the stealthy hippopotamus, and likewise of the six-toed Wallipaloova bird, that hides himself under

Courtesy Ruth Koerner Oliver

Holding the Herd

his wing," said Dines. "I've never been in Hillsboro, and I never saw your girl. But when you write her a letter addressed to yourself—why don't your dad take that letter home and keep it till you come? How is she going to get it out of the post office? She can't—unless she works in the post office herself. Old man Seiber is postmaster at Hillsboro. I've heard that much. And he's got a daughter named Kitty. You see now I was telling you true—you talk too much."

Weir's face went scarlet with rage.

"Here's a fine how-de-do about a damn little—"

That word was never uttered. Johnny's horse, with rein and knee and spur to guide and goad, reared high and flung sidewise. White hoofs flashed above Weir's startled eyes; Johnny launched himself through the air straight at Jody's throat. Johnny's horse fell crashing after, twisting, bestriding at once the other horse and the two locked and straining men. Weir's horse floundered and went down, men and horses rolled together in the sand. From first to last you might have counted—one—two—three—four! Johnny came clear of the tangle with Jody's six-shooter in his hand. He grabbed Jody by the collar and dragged him from under the struggling horses.

"We can't go on with this, Jody!" he said gravely. "You've got no gun!"

II

" 'She is useful to us, undoubtedly,' answered Corneuse, 'but she does us an injury by ruining us.' "
— *The Elm Tree on the Mall.*

THE Jornada is a high desert of table-land, east of the Rio Grande. In design it is strikingly like a billiard table; forty-five miles by ninety, with mountain ranges for rail at east and west, broken highlands on the south, a lava bed on the north. At the middle of each rail and at each corner, for pockets, there is a mountain passway and water; there are peaks and landmarks for each diamond on the rail; for the center and for each spot there is a railroad station and water —Lava, Engle and Upham. Roughly speaking there is road or trail from each spot to each pocket, each spot to each spot, each pocket to every other pocket. In the center, where you put the pin at pin pool, stands Engle.

Noon of the next day found Johnny nearing Moongate Pass, a deep notch in the San Andreas Mountains; a smooth semicircle ex-

31

actly filled and fitted by the rising moon, when full and seen from Engle. Through Moongate led the wagon road, branching at the high parks on the summit to five springs: The Bar Cross horse camp, Bear Den, Rosebud, Good Fortune, Grapevine.

Johnny drove his casualties slowly up the gentle valley. On either hand a black-cedared ridge climbed eastward, each to a high black mountain at the head of the pass. Johnny gathered up what saddle horses were in the pass and moved them along with his cripples.

At the summit he came to a great gateway country of parks and cedar mottes, gentle slopes and low rolling ridges, with wide smooth valleys falling away to north and south; eastward rose a barrier of red-sandstone hills. High in those red hills Johnny saw two horsemen. They drove a bunch of horses of their own; they rode swiftly down a winding backbone to intercept him. He held up his little herd; the two riders slowed up in response. They came through a greenwood archway to the little cove where Johnny waited. One was a boy of sixteen, Bob Gifford, left in charge of the horse camp; the other a tall stranger who held up his hand in salute. Young Bob reined up with a gay flourish.

"Hello, Dinesy!" He took a swift survey of Johnny's little herd and sized up the situation. "Looks like you done signed up with the Bar Cross."

"Oh, *si!* Here's a list of horses Cole sent for. I don't know 'em all, so I brought along all I saw."

Bob took the scrap of paper.

"Calabaza, Jug, Silver Dick—Oh, excuse me! Mr. Hales, this is Johnny Dines. Mr. Hales is thinkin' some of buying that ornery Spot horse of mine. Johnny, you got nigh all you need to make good your hospital list. Now let's see. Um-m!—Twilight, Cyclone, Dynamite, Rebel, Sif Sam, Cigarette, Skyrocket, Straight-edge, and so forth, Um! Your mount, that bunch? Sweet spirits of nitre! Oh, cowboy! You sure got to ride!"

"Last man takes the leavings," said Johnny.

"You got 'em." Bob rolled his eyes eloquently. "I'll tell a man! Two sticks and eleven catawampouses! Well, it's your funeral. Any rush?"

"Just so I get back to Engle to-morrow night."

"Easy as silk, then. All them you ain't got here will be in to water to-night or to-morrow morning, 'cept Bluebeard and Popcorn. They run at Puddingstone Tanks, down the cañon. You and me will go get 'em after dinner."

"Dinner? Let's go! Got any beef, Bobby?"

"Better'n beef. Bear meat—jerked. Make hair grow on your chest. Ever eat any?"

"Bear meat? Who killed a bear?"

"Me. Little Bobby. All alone. Three of 'em. Killed three in the yard the very first morning," said little Bobby proudly. "I heard them snuffin' and millin' round out in the water pen in the night, but I thought it was stock. Then they come up in the house yard. Soon as it come day I got up to drive 'em out—and behold you, they was no stock, but three whoppin' brown bears. So I fogged 'em. Killed all three before they could get out of the yard."

"Good Lord!" said Johnny. His face drooped to troubled lines. The man Hales glanced sharply at him.

"Heap big chief me!" prattled Bobby, unnoting. "Two bully good skins—had to shoot the last one all to rags to kill him—and twelve hundred pounds of good meat. Wah!" He turned to the stranger. "Well, Mr. Hales, do you think that little old plug of mine will suit you?"

"Oh, I reckon so. Beggars mustn't be choosers—and I sure need him. Thirty dollars, you said?"

"Wouldn't take a cent more. I'm not gougin' you. That's his price, weekdays or Sunday. He don't look much, but he ain't such a bad little hoss."

Hales nodded. "He'll do, I guess."

"You done bought a horse!" said Bobby. "And Johnny, he's got a mount to make him a rep—if they don't spill him." He broke into rollicking song:

They picked me up and carried me in;
They rubbed me down with a rolling pin.
"Oh, that's the way we all begin,
    You're doing well," says Brown;
"To-morrow morn, if you don't die,
I'll give you another horse to try."
"Oh, can't you let me walk?" says I ——

Here he cocked an impish eye at Dines, observed that gentleman's mournful face, and broke the song short.

"What's the matter with you now, Dinesy? You can ride 'em, of course. No trouble after you first take the edge off."

"It isn't that," said Dines sorrowfully. "I —I—you ain't a bit to blame, but—"

He stopped, embarrassed.

"What's the matter, you old fool? Spill it!"

Johnny sighed and drew in a long breath.

"I hate to name it, Bob—I do so. Hiram Yoast and Foamy White, the blamed old fools, they orter told you! They'll be all broke up about this." He looked Bob square in the eye and plunged on desperately. "Them bears, Bobby—Hiram and Foamy had been makin' pets of 'em. Feedin' them beef bones and such ever since last spring—had 'em plumb gentle."

"Hell and damnation!"

Johnny's eyes were candid and compassionate. "Anybody would have done just the same, Bobby. Don't you feel too bad about it. Rotten durned shame, though. Them bears was a bushel o' fun. Jack and Jill, the two biggest ones, they was a leetle mite stand-offish and inclined to play it safe. But the Prodigal Son, that's the least one—growed a heap since last spring with plenty to eat that way—why, the Prodigal he'd never met up with any man but Foamy and Hi, so he wasn't a mite leery. Regular clown, that bear. Stand up right in front of the door, and catch biscuit and truck the boys threw to him—loll out his little red tongue and grin like a house afire. He was right comical. How he did love molasses!"

"How come them fools didn't tell me?" demanded the crestfallen hunter, almost in tears.

"Pretty tough luck," said Hales commiseratingly. "I killed a pet deer once. I know just how you feel."

"I don't know who's to break it to Hiram and Foamy," said Johnny, grieving. "It's goin' to hurt 'em, bad! They set a heap of store by them bears—'special the Prodigal— poor little fellow! I feel right bad myself, and I was only here two nights. Make it all the worse for them, being all on account of their cussed carelessness. I can't see how you're a bit to blame. Only I do think you might have noticed your night horse didn't make any fuss. Usual, horses are scared stiff of bears. But they'd got plumb used to these."

"Didn't keep up no horse that night," said Bob miserably.

"Look here!" said Hales. "What's the use of letting them other fellows know anything about it? Mr. Dines and me, we won't tell. This young man can send his bearskins over east, Tularosa or somewhere, and keep his lip buttoned up. No one need be ever the wiser. Bears change their range whenever they get good and ready. Nobody need know but what they just took a notion to light out."

"Say, that's the right idea!" said Johnny, brightening. "That'll save a heap of trouble.

Boys are liable to think the round-up scared 'em out—as might happen, easy. That ain't all either. That plan will not only save Hi and Foamy a heap o' grief, but it won't be no bad thing for Bob Gifford. I'll tell you honest, Bob—the Bar Cross will near devil the life out of you if this thing ever gets out."

"That's good dope, kid," said Hales kindly. "No use cryin' over spilt milk."

"Let's drop it then. I'll get rid of the bear hides."

"That's right. Talkin' about it only makes you feel bad. Forget it. Here, I'll give you something else to think about. You two seem to be all right."

Hales drew rein, with a long appraising look at the younger man. It seemed to satisfy him; he rode a little to one side, facing a wooded sugar-loaf hill in the middle of the rough gap leading east to Rosebud. He waved his hand. A crackling of brush made instant answer; high above them a horseman came from cover and picked his way down the steep hill.

"Friend of mine," explained Hales, returning. "He is sort of watering at night, just now. No hanging matter—but he wouldn't have showed up unless I waved him the O. K. And he is sure one hungry man. It's for him I bought the horse."

Johnny reflected a little. This was no new or startling procedure. Besides being the most lonesome spot in a thinly settled country, with a desert on each side, and with Engle, thirty miles, for next neighbor, the horse camp had other advantages. It was situated in the Panhandle of Socorro County; a long, thin strip of rough mountain, two townships wide and five long, with Sierra County west, Dona Ana to the south, Lincoln and Otero on the east; a convenient juxtaposition in certain contingencies. Many gentlemen came uncommunicative to the horse camp and departed unquestioned. In such case the tradition of hospitality required the host to ride afield against the parting time; so being enabled to say truly that he knew not the direction of his guest's departure. Word was passed on; the Panhandle became well and widely known;

we all know what the lame dog did to the doctor.

But Johnny rubbed his nose. This thing had been done with needless ostentation; and Johnny did not like Mr. Hales' face. It was a furtive face; the angles of the eyes did not quite match, so that the eyes seemed to keep watch of each other; moreover, they were squinched little eyes, and set too close to the nose; the nose was too thin and was pinched to a covert sneer, aided therein by a sullen mouth under heavy mustaches. Altogether Mr. Hales did not look like a man overgiven to trustfulness. Johnny did not see any reason why Mr. Hales' friend should not have ridden in later and with more reticence; so he set himself to watch for such reason.

"My friend, Mr. Smith," announced Hales, as Mr. Smith joined them. Mr. Smith, like the others, wore belt and six-shooter; also, a rifle was strapped under his knee. He was a short and heavy-set man, singularly carefree of appearance, and he now inquired with great earnestness: "Anybody mention grub?"

"Sure," said Bobby. "Let's drift! Only a mile or so."

> *We all went to the ranch next day;*
> *Brown augured me most all the way;*
> *He said cowpunching was only play,*
>   *There was no work at all.*
> *"All you have to do is ride,*
>   *It's just like drifting with the tide ——"*
> *Lord have mercy, how he lied!*
>   *He had a most horrible gall!*

The walling hills were higher now. The cañon fell away swiftly to downward plunge, gravel between cut banks. Just above the horse camp it made a sharp double-S curve. Riding across a short cut of shoulder, Bob, in the lead, held up a hand to check the others. He rode up on a little platform to the right, from which, as pedestal, rose a great hill of red sandstone, square-topped and incredibly steep. Bobby waved his hat; a man on foot appeared on the crest of the red hill and zig-zagged down the steeps. He wore a steeple-crowned hat and he carried a long rifle in the crook of his arm.

Johnny's eyes widened. He exchanged a

Courtesy Ruth Koerner Oliver

Bobby

glance with Hales; and he observed that Smith and Hales did not look at each other. Yet they had—so Johnny thought—one brief glance coming to them, under the circumstances.

Hales pitched his voice low.

"You was lying about them bears, of course?"

"Got to keep boys in their place," said Johnny in the same guarded undertone. "If them bears had really been pets do you suppose I'd ever have opened my head about it?"

"It went down easy." Hales grinned his admiration. "You taken one chance though —about his night horse."

"Not being scared, you mean? Well, he hasn't mentioned any horse having a fit. And I reckoned maybe he hadn't kept up any night horse. Really nothing much for him to do. Except cooking."

"He does seem to have a right smart of company," agreed Hales.

Bob returned with the last comer—a gaunt, brown man with a gift for silence.

"My friend, Mr. Jones," Bob explained

gravely. "He stakes his horse on that hilltop. Bully grass there. And quiet. He likes quiet. He doesn't care for strangers a-tall—not unless I stand good for 'em."

The camp—a single room, some fourteen feet by eighteen, flat roofed, made of stone with a soapstone fireplace—was built in a fenced yard on a little low red flat, looped about by the cañon, pleasant with shady cedars, overhung by a red and mighty mountain at the back, faced by a mightier mountain of white limestone. The spring gushed out at the contact of red and white.

The bunch of saddle horses was shut up in the water pen. Preparation for dinner went forward merrily, not without favorable comment from Mr. Smith for Bob's three bearskins, a proud carpet on the floor. Mr. Jones had seen them before; Hales and Johnny kept honorable silence on that theme. Hales and Mr. Smith set a good example by removing belt and gun; an example followed by Bob, but by neither Johnny nor Mr. Jones. The latter gentleman indeed had leaned his rifle in the corner beyond the table. But while the discussion of bearskins was most animated, Johnny caught Mr. Jones' eye, and arched a brow. Johnny next took occasion to roll his own eye slowly at the unconscious backs of Mr. Hales and Mr. Smith—and then transferred his gaze, very pointedly, to the long rifle in the corner. Shortly after, Mr. Jones rose and took a seat behind the table, with the long rifle at his right hand.

"Well, Mr. Bob," said Hales when dinner was over, "here's your thirty dollars. You give Smith a bill of sale and get your pardner to witness it. Me, I'm telling you good-by. I'm due to lead Smith's discard pony about forty mile north to-night, and set him loose about daylight—up near the White Oaks stage road. Thank'ee kindly. Good-by, all!"

"Wait a minute, Toad," said Smith briskly. "I'll catch up my new cayuse and side you a little ways. Stake him out in good grass, some quiet place—like my pardner here." He grinned at Mr. Jones, who smiled, attentive. "I'll hang my saddle in a tree and hoof it back about dark. Safe enough here—all good fellows. And I sure like that bear meat.

To say nothing of being full up of myself for society."

"We'll do the dishes," said Johnny. "Bob, you rope me up the gentlest of my hyenas and we'll slip down to Puddingstone presently."

"Well, good luck to you, Mr. Dines," said Hales at the door.

"So long."

"That horse you've got staked out, Mr. Jones," said Johnny, when the others were catching horses, "how about him? I've got a private horse out in the water pen. Shall we swap? Saddles too? You're a little the biggest, but you can let out my stirrups a notch, and I can take up a notch in yours, up on that pinnacle when I go for my new horse and come back—about dark. That way, you might ride down the cañon with Bob. I think maybe—if it was important—Bob might not find the horses he wants, and might lay out to-night. And you might tell him you was coming back to camp. But you can always change your mind, you know. 'All you have to do is ride.'"

"This is right clever of you, young man," said Jones slowly.

"It sure is. Your saddle any good?"

"Better'n yours. Enough better to make up for the difference in hosses, unless yours is a jo-darter. My hoss is tired."

"He'll have all fall to rest up. We'd better trade hats, too. Somebody might be watchin' from the hills."

"Them fellows?" Jones motioned toward the water pen with the plate he was drying.

"Scouts, I guess. Decoy ducks. More men close, I judge. Acted like it. You ought to know."

"It ain't noways customary to send two men after me," said Jones.

Johnny nodded. "You don't know about Smithy yet. Let me wise you up." He outlined the trustfulness of Smithy. "So he was all labeled up for an outlaw, like a sandwich man. Putting one over on Bobby—him being a boy. Bobby fell for it. And me, just a big kid myself, what show did I have with two big grown men smooth as all that? So they fooled me, too. Smithy said 'Toad' once—notice? Toad Hales. I've heard of Toad Hales. Socorro way. Big mitt man, once. Skunk—but no fighting fool. Out for the dollar."

"He sees some several. You're takin' right smart of a chance, young fellow."

"I guess I've got a right to swap horses if I want to. Hark! They're ridin' up the cañon."

"Well, suh, I'm right obliged to you, and that's a fact."

"I'm not doing this for you exactly. I'm protectin' the Bar Cross. And that's funny, too," said Johnny. "I've just barely signed up with the outfit, and right off things begin to take place in great lumps and gobs. More action in two days than I've seen before in two years. Here's how I look at it: If anyone sees fit to ride up on you and gather you on the square I've got nothing to say. But I hold no candle to treachery. You're here under trust. I owe it to the Bar Cross—and to you —that you leave here no worse off than you came. I don't know what you've done. If it's mean enough, I may owe it to Johnny Dines to go after you myself later on. But you go safe from here first. That's my job."

"And I'll bet you'd sure come a-snuffin'. I judge you're a right white man, suh! But it's not so mean as all that, this time. Not even a case of 'alive or dead.' Just 'for arrest and conviction.' So I guess you'll be reasonably safe on the hillside. No money in killing you, or me, or whoever brings my hoss off of that hill. And they'll be counting on gathering you in easy—asleep here, likely."

"That's the way I figured it—that last."

"But how'll you square yourself with the sheriff?"

"I'll contrive to make strap and buckle meet some way. Man dear, I've got to!"

"Well, then—I owe you a day in harvest. Good-by, suh. Jones, he pulls his freight."

Johnny brought his new horse and saddle down from the red hill, unmolested. He cut out what horses he wanted to keep in the branding pen; turned the others loose, his new acquisition with them; and started supper.

Mr. Smith joined him at dark; but the horse hunters did not get back. Supper followed, then seven-up and conversation. Johnny fretted over the non-return of Gifford.

"He talked as if he knew right where to lay his hand on them horses," he complained. "Wish I had gone myself. Now in the morning I'll have to be out of here at daylight. That bunch I got in the pen, I got to take them out to grass, and wait till Bob comes— if the blame little fool sleeps out to-night."

"Oh, he'll be in purty quick, likely."

"I don't know," said Johnny dejectedly. "I had to-morrow all figured out like a time-table, and here it's all gummed up. Listen. What's that in the yard—crunchin'? Varmints, likely. When I was here last we used to throw out beef bones, and of nights we'd shoot through the doorway at the noise. We got eight skunks and three coyotes and a fox and a tub. Guess I'll try a shot now." He picked up his revolver and cocked it.

"Hello, the house!" said a hurried voice outside.

"Why, it's a man!" said Johnny. He

turned his gun upon Mr. Smith. "One word and you're done," he whispered. His eye was convincing. Smith petrified. Johnny raised his voice. "Hello, outside! You come near getting shot for a skunk! If you want supper and shelter say please and walk out loud like a man. I don't like your pussy-foot ways."

"Come out of there—one at a time—hands up!" said the voice. "We've got you surrounded. You can't get away!"

"On the contrary, we are behind thick walls, and you can get away if you're right quick and immediate," said Johnny. "Inside of a minute I'm going to empty a rifle out there on general principles. This is a Bar Cross house. I am a Bar Cross man, where I belong, following orders. Half a minute more!"

"You fool! This is the sheriff's posse!"

"I hear you say it."

"I am the sheriff of Socorro County," said another voice, "and I summon you to surrender."

"I am a Bar Cross man in a Bar Cross

house," repeated Johnny. "If you're the sheriff, walk in that door on your hind legs, with your hands up, and let us have a look at you."

"That's Johnny Dines talking!" said a third voice. "Hello, Dines! This is me, Bill Fewell! Say, this is the sheriff and his posse all right! Don't you get in wrong."

"One man may unbuckle his belt and back in at that door, hands up. If you can show any papers for me, I surrender. While I give 'em the quick look, the man that comes in is a hostage with my gun between his shoulder blades. If he takes his hands down or anybody tries any funny business, I'll make a sieve of him. Step lively!"

"Dines, you fool," bawled the sheriff, "I got nothing against you. But I've got a warrant for that man in there with you, and I'm going to have him."

"Oh!" A moment's silence. Then said Johnny, in an injured voice: "You might ha' said so before. I've got him covered and I've taken his gun. So now I've got one gun for him and one for the hostage. Send in one man walking backward, hands up, warrant in his belt—and let him stop right in the door! No mistakes. If the warrant is right you get your man. Any reward?"

"He's a stiff-necked piece," said Fewell. "But he'll do just what he says. Here, give me your warrant. He won't hurt me—if you fellows hold steady. If you don't, you've murdered me, that's all. Hey, Dines! You stubborn long-eared Missouri mule, I'm coming, as per instructions—me, Bill Fewell. You be careful!"

He backed up and stood framed in the open door against the lamplight. Johnny's hand flickered out and snatched the warrant.

"Why, sheriff, this seems to be all right. Only he gave me a different name. But then, he naturally would. Why, this warrant is all shipshape. Hope I get some of that reward. Here's your man, and here are my guns." He appeared at the door and tossed his guns down. The sheriff crowded by, and broke into a bellow of rage.

"You fool! You blundering idiot! This is one of my posse!"

"What?" Johnny's jaw dropped in pained surprise. "He's a liar, then. He told me he was an outlaw. Don't blame me!"

"You hell-sent half-wit! Where's that other man—Jones?"

"Oh, him? He's down the cañon, sir. He went with Bob after horses. He hasn't got back yet, sir."

"Dines, you scoundrel! Are you trying to make a fool out of me?"

"Oh, no, sir! Impossible. Not at all, sir. If you and your posse will take cover, sir, I'll capture him for you when he comes back, just as I did this one, sir. We are always glad to use the Bar Cross house as a trap and the Bar Cross grub for bait. As you see, sir."

"Damn you, Dines, that man isn't coming back!"

Johnny considered this for a little. Then he looked up with innocent eyes.

"Perhaps you are right, sir," he said thoughtfully.

Long since, the floods have washed out the Bar Cross horse camp, torn away pens and flat and house, leaving from hill to hill a desolate wash of gravel and boulders—so that no man may say where that poor room stood. Yet youth housed there and hope, honor and courage and loyalty; there are those who are glad it shall shelter no meaner thing.

III

"I do believe there shall be a winter yet in heaven—and in hell."
　　　　　　　　　　　　　　—*Paradise and the Periscope.*

"Realism, *n.* The art of depicting nature as it is seen by toads."
　　　　　　　　　　　　　　—*The Devil's Dictionary.*

"They sit brooding on a garbage scow and tell us how bad the world smells."
　　　　　　　　　　　　　　—Berton Braley.

"JUST round the block" is a phrase familiar to you. To get the same effect in the open country you would say "Thirty miles" or sixty; and in those miles it is likely there would be no water and no house—perhaps not any tree. Consider now: Within the borders of New Mexico might be poured New York, New Jersey, Pennsylvania, Maryland, Delaware. Then drop in another small state and all of Chesapeake Bay, and still New Mexico would not be brimful—though it would have to be carried carefully to avoid slopping over. Scattered across this country is a population less than that of Buffalo—half of it clustered in six-mile ribbons along the Rio Grande and the Pecos. Those figures are for to-day. Divide them by three, and then excuse the story if it steps round the block. It was long ago; Plancus was consul then.

Some two weeks after the day when Johnny Dines went to horse camp, Charlie See rode northward through the golden September; northward from Rincon, pocket of that billiard table you know of. His way was east of the Rio Grande, in the desperate twisting country where the river cuts through Caballo Mountains. His home was beyond the river, below Rincon, behind Cerro Roblado and Selden Hill; and he rode for a reason he had. Not for the first time; at every farm and clearing he was hailed with greeting and jest.

Across the river he saw the yellow walls of Colorado, of old Fort Thorne, deserted Santa Barbara. He came abreast of them, left them behind, came to Wit's End, where the river gnaws at the long bare ridges and the wagon road clings and clambers along the brown hillside. He rode sidewise and swaying, crooning a gay little saddle song; to which Stargazer, his horse, twitched back an inquiring ear.

Oh, there was a crooked man and he rode a crooked mile ——

Charlie See was as straight as his own rifle; it was the road he traveled which prompted that joyful saddle song. As will be found upon examination, that roistering ditty sorts with a joyful jog trot. It follows that Charlie See was not riding at a run, as frontiersmen do in the movies. It is a great and neglected truth that frontiersmen on the frontier never ride like the frontiersmen in films. And it may be mentioned in passing that frontiersmen on frontiers never do anything at all resembling as to motive, method or result those things which frontiersmen do in films. And that is the truth.

The actual facts are quite simple and jolly. In pursuit of wild stock, men run their horses at top speed for as short a time as may be contrived; not to make the wild stock run faster and farther, but to hold up the wild stock. Once checked, they proceed as soberly as may be to the day's destination; eventually to a market. Horse or steer comes to market in good shape or bad, as the handling has been reckless or tender; and the best cowman is he whose herds have been moved slowest. At exceptional times—riding with or from the sheriff, to get a doctor, or, for a young man in April, riding a fresh horse for a known and measured distance, speed is permitted. But the rule is to ride slowly and sedately, holding swiftness in reserve for need. Walk, running walk, pace, jog trot—those are the road gaits, to which horses are carefully trained, giving most mileage with least effort. Rack and single-foot are tolerated but frowningly.

The mad, glad gallop is reserved for childhood and for emergencies. Penalties, progressively suitable, are provided for the mad, glad galloper. He becomes the object of sidelong glances and meaning smiles; persistent, he becomes the theme of gibe and jest to flay the skin. If he be such a one as would neither observe nor forecast, one who will neither learn nor be taught, soon or late he finds himself set afoot with a give-out horse; say, twenty-five miles from water. It is not on record that wise or foolish, after one such experience, is ever partial to the sprightly gallop as a road gait. Of thirst, as of "eloquent, just and mightie Death," it may be truly said: "Whom none could advise, thou hast perswaded."

The road wound down to the bottom land for a little space. Then sang Charlie See:

> *Oh, mind you not in yonder town*
> *When the red wine you were fillin',*
> *You drank a health to the ladies round*
> *And slighted Barbara Allan?*

Followed a merry ditty of old days:

> *Foot in the stirrup and a hand on the horn,*
> *Best old cowboy ever was born!*
> *Hi, yi-yippy, yippy-hi-yi-yi,*
> *Hi-yi-yippy-yippy-yay!*

> *Stray in the herd and the boss said kill it,*
> *Shot him in the ear with the handle of the skillet!*
> *Hi, yi-yippy, yippy-hi-yi-yi,*
> *Hi-yi-yippy-yippy-yay!*

That rollicking chorus died away. The wagon road turned up a sandy draw for a

long detour, to cross the high ridges far inland. Stargazer clambered up the Drunkard's Mile, a steep and dizzy cut-off. High
on an overhang of halfway shelf, between
water and sky, Stargazer paused for breathing
space.

> *The world has no place for a dreamer of dreams,*
> *Then 'tis no place for me, it seems,*
> *Dearie! . . . My dearie!*

Echo rang bugle-brave from cliff to cliff,
pealed exulting, answered again—came back
long after, faint and far:
"Dearie! . . . My dearie!"
He looked down, musing, at the swirling
black waters far below.

> *For I dream of you all the day long!*
> *You run through the hours like a song!*
> *Nothing's worth while save dreams of you,*
> *And you can make every dream come true—*
> *Dearie!   My dearie!*

Drunkard's Mile fell off into the valley at
Redbrush and joined the wagon road there.
They passed Beck's Ferry and Beneteau's;
they came to a bridge over the *acequia madre,*

the mother ditch, wide and deep. Beyond
was a wide valley of cleared and irrigated
farm lands. This was Garfield settlement.

. . . .

You remember Mr. Dick and how he could
not keep King Charles' head out of his
Memorial? A like unhappiness is mine.
When I remember that pleasant settlement
as it really was, cheerful and busy and merry,
I am forced to think how gleefully the super-
sophisticated Sons of Light would fall afoul
of these friendly folk—how they would pounce
upon them with jeering laughter, scoff at their
simple joys and fears; set down, with heavy
and hateful satisfaction, every lack and long-
ing; flout at each brave makeshift, such as
Little Miss Brag crowed over, jubilant, when
she pointed with pride:

> *For little Miss Brag, she lays much stress*
> *On the privileges of a gingham dress—*
> *A-ha-a! O-ho-o!*

A lump comes to my throat, remembering;
now my way is plain; if I would not be in-
comparably base, I must speak up for my own

people. Now, like Mr. Dick, I must fly my kite, with these scraps and tags of Memorial. The string is long, and if the kite flies high it may take the facts a long way; the winds must bear them as they will.

Consider now the spreading gospel of despair, and marvel at the power of words—noises in the air, marks upon paper. Let us wonder to see how little wit is needed to twist and distort truth that it may set forth a lie. A tumblebug zest, a nose pinched to sneering, a slurring tongue—with no more equipment you and I could draw a picture of Garfield as it is done in the fashion of to-day.

Be blind and deaf to help and hope, gay courage, hardship nobly borne; appeal to envy, greed, covetousness; belaud extravagance and luxury; magnify every drawback; exclaim at rude homes, simple dress, plain food, manners not copied from imitators of Europe's idlesse; use ever the mean and mocking word—how easy to belittle! Behold Garfield—barbarous, uncouth, dreary, desolate, savage and forlorn; there misery kennels, huddled between jungle and moaning waste; there, lout and boor crouch in their wretched hovels! We have left out little; only the peace of mighty mountains far and splendid, a gallant sun and the illimitable sky, tingling and eager life, and the invincible spirit of man.

Such picture as this of Garfield *comme il faut* is, I humbly conceive, what a great man, who trod earth bravely, had in mind when he wondered at "the spectral unreality of realistic books." It is what he forswore in his up-summing: "And the true realism is . . . to find out where joy resides and give it a voice beyond singing."

This trouble about Charles the First and our head—it started in 1645, I think—needs looking into.

There are circles where "adventurer" is a term of reproach, where "romance" is made synonym for a lie, and a silly lie at that. Curious! The very kernel and meaning of romance is the overcoming of difficulties or a manly constancy of striving; a strong play pushed home or defeat well borne. And it would be hard to find a man but found his own life a breathless adventure, brief and hard, with ups and downs enough, strivings through all defeats.

Interesting, if true. But can we prove this? Certainly—by trying. Mr. Dick sets us all right. Put any man to talk of what he knows best—corn, coal or lumber—and hear matters throbbing with the entrancing interest born only of first-hand knowledge. Our pessimists "suspect nothing but what they do not understand, and they suspect everything"—as was said of the commission set to judge the regicides who cut off the head of Charles the Martyr—whom I may have mentioned, perhaps.

Let the dullest man tell of the thing he knows at first hand, and his speech shall tingle with battle and luck and loss, purr for small comforts of cakes and ale or sound the bell note of clean mirth; his voice shall exult with pride of work, tingle and tense to speak of hard-won steeps, the burden and heat of the day and "the bright face of danger"; it shall be soft as quiet water to tell of shadows where winds loiter, of moon magic and far-off suns, friendship and fire and song. There will be more, too, which he may not say, having no words. We prate of little things, each to each; but we fall silent before love and death.

It was once commonly understood that it is not good for a man to whine. Only of late has it been discovered that a thinker is superficial and shallow unless he whines; that no man is wise unless he views with alarm. Eager propaganda has disseminated the glad news that everything is going to the demnition bowwows. Willing hands pass on the word. The method is simple. They write very long books in which they set down the evil on the one side—and nothing on the other. That is "realism." Whatsoever things are false, whatsoever things are dishonest, whatsoever things are unjust, whatsoever things are impure, whatsoever things are of ill report; if there be any vice, and if there be any shame —they think on these things. They gloat upon these things; they wallow in these things.

The next time you hanker for a gripping, stinging, roaring romance, try the story of

Eddystone Lighthouse.   There wasn't a realist on the job—they couldn't stand the gaff.   For any tough lay like this of Winstanley's dream you want a gang of idealists—the impractical kind.   It is not a dismal story; it is a long record of trouble, delay, setbacks, exposure, hardship, death and danger, failure, humiliation, jeers, disaster and ruin.   Crippled idealists were common in Plymouth Harbor. The sea and the wind mocked their labor; they were crushed, frozen and drowned; but they built Eddystone Light!   And men in other harbors took heart again to build great lights against night and storm; the world over, realists fare safelier on the sea for Winstanley's dream.

There is the great distinction between realism and reality: It is the business of a realist to preach how man is mastered by circumstances; it is the business of a man to prove that he will be damned first.

You may note this curious fact of dismal books—that you remember no passage to quote to your friends.   Not one.   And you perceive, with lively astonishment, that despairing books are written by the fortunate. The homespun are not so easily discouraged. When crows pull up their corn they do not quarrel with Creation. They comment on the crows, and plant more corn.

This trouble in King Charles' head may be explained, in part, on a closer looking. As for those who announce the bankruptcy of an insolvent and wildcat universe, with no extradition, and who proclaim God the Great Absconder—they are mostly of the emerged tenth. Their lips do curl with scorn; and what they scorn most is work—and doers. For what they deign to praise—observe, sir, for yourself, what they uphold, directly or by implication. See if it be not a thing compact of graces possible only to idleness. See if it be not their great and fatal mistake that they regard culture as an end in itself, and not as a means for service. Aristocracy? Patricians? In a world which has known the tinker of Bedford, the druggist's clerk of Edmonton, the Stratford poacher, backwoods Lincoln, a thousand others, and ten thousand —a carpenter's son among them?

Returning to the Provisional Government: Regard its members closely, these gods *ad interim*. The ground of their depression is that everybody is not Just like Them. They have a grievance also in the matter of death; which might have been arranged better. It saddens them to know that so much excellence as theirs should perish from the earth. The skeptic is slacker, too; excusing himself from the hardships of right living by pleading the futility of effort.

Unfair? Of course I am unfair; all this is assumption without knowledge, a malicious imputation of the worst possible motives, judgment from a part. It is their own method.

A wise word was said of late: "There are poor colonels, but no poor regiments." It would be truer to change a word; to say that there are poor soldiers, but no poor regiments. The gloomster picks the poorest soldier he can find, and holds him up to our eyes as a sample. "This is life!" says the pessimist, proud at last. "Now you see the stuff your regiments are made of!"

If one of these pallbearers should write a treatise on pomology he would dwell lovingly on apple-tree borers, blight and pest and scale. He would say no word of spray or pruning; he would scoff at the glory of apple blossoms as the rosy illusion of romance; and he would resolutely suppress all mention of—apples. But he would feature hard cider, for all that; and he would revel in cankerworms.

These blighters and borers—figuratively speaking—when the curse of the bottle is upon them—the ink bottle—they weave ugly words to ugly phrases for ugly books about ugly things; with ugly thoughts of ugly deeds they chronicle life and men as dreary, sordid, base, squalid, paltry, tawdry, mean, dismal, dull and dull again, interminably dull—vile, flat, stale, unprofitable and insipid. No splendid folly or valiant sin—much less impracticable ideal-isms, such as kindness, generosity, faith, for-giveness, courage, honor, friendship, love; no charm or joy or beauty, no ardors that flame and glow. They show forth a world of beast-liness and bankruptcy; they picture life as a purposeless hell.

I beg of you, sir, do not permit yourself to be alarmed. What you hear is but the back-door gossip of the world. And these people do not get enough exercise. Their livers are torpid. Some of them, poor fellows, are quite sincere—and some are merely in the fashion. It isn't true, you know; not of all of us, all the time. Nothing is changed; there is no shadow but proves the light; in the farthest world of any universe, in the latest eternity you choose to mention, it will still be playing the game to run out your hits; and there, as here, only the shirker will lie down on the job.

In the meantime, now and here, there are two things, and two only, that a man may do with his ideals: He may hold and shape them, or tread them under foot; ripen or rot.

What, sir, the hills are steep, the sand heavy, the mire is Despond-deep; for that reason will you choose a balky horse? Or will you follow a leader who plans surrender?

The bookshelviki have thrown away the sword before the fight. They shriek a shameful message: "All is lost! Save yourselves who can!"

The battle is sore upon us; true. But there is another war cry than this. It was born of a bitter hour; it was nobly boasted, and brave men made it good. Now, and for all time to come, as the lost and furious fight reels by, men will turn and turn again for the watchword of Verdun: "They shall not pass! They shall not pass!"

Pardon the pontifical character of these remarks. They come tardy off. For years I have kept a safe and shameful silence when I should have been shouting, "Janet! Donkeys!" and throwing things. I will be highbrow-beaten no longer. I hereby resign from the choir inaudible. Modesty may go hang and prudence be jiggered; I wear Little Miss Brag's colors for favor; I have cut me an ellum gad, and I mean to use it on the seat of the scorner.

"Everything in Nature is engaged in writing its own history." So says Emerson or somebody. Here is the roll call of that lonesome bit between the Rio Grande and Caballo Mountain. Salem, Garfield, Donahue's,

Derry and Shandon; those were the hamlets of the east side. Sound Irish, don't they? They were just what they sound like, at first. A few Irish families, big families, half of them girls—Irish girls; young gentlemen with a fancy to settle down settled right there or thereabouts. That's a quick way to start settlements. There was also a sardonic Greenhorn, to keep alive a memory of the old-time Texans, before the fences. A hundred years older than Greenhorn was the old Mexican outpost, San Ysidro; ruthlessly changed to Garfield when the Mississippi Valley moved in. Transportation was the poorest ever; this was the last-won farm land of New Mexico.

Along with snakes, centipedes, little yellow bobcats, whisky, poker, maybe a beef or two —there were other features worthy of note. Each man had to be cook, housekeeper, hunter, laundryman, shoemaker, blacksmith, bookkeeper, purchasing agent, miner, mason, nurse, doctor, gravedigger, interpreter, surveyor, tailor, jailor, judge, jury and sheriff. Having no sea handy, he was seldom a sailorman.

A man who could do these things well

enough to make them work might be illiterate, but he couldn't be ignorant, not on a bet. It wasn't possible. He knew too much. He had to do his own thinking. There was no one else to do it for him. And he could not be wretched. He was too busy. "We may be poor sinners, but we're not miserable"—that was a favorite saying. When they brought in supplies or when they packed for a long trip, they learned foresight and imagination. A right good college, the frontier; there are many who are proud of that degree.

It is easy to be hospitable, kindly and free-hearted in a thinly settled country; it is your turn next, you know generosity from both sides; the Golden Rule has no chance to get rusty. So they were pleasant and friendly people. They learned coöperation by making wagon roads together, by making dams and big irrigation ditches, and from the round-ups. They lived in the open air, and their work was hard, they had health; there were endless difficulties to overcome; happiness had a long start and the pursuit was merry.

There was one other great advantage—

hope. They had much to hope for. Almost
everything. They wished three great wishes;
Water for the fields, safety from floods, a way
to the outside world. To-day the thick and
tangled *bosques* are cleared to smiling farms,
linked by a shining network of ditches. The
floods are impounded at Engle Dam, and held
there for man's uses. A great irrigation canal
keeps high and wide, with just fall enough to
move the water; each foot saved of high level
means added miles of reclaimed land under
the ditch. To a stranger's eye the water of
that ditch runs clearly uphill. To hold that
high level the main ditch, which is first taken
out to serve the west side, crosses the Rio
Grande on a high flume to Derry; curves high
and winding about the wide farm lands of
Garfield valley; is siphoned under the river
for Hatch and Rodey, and then is siphoned
once again to the east side, to break out in the
sunlight for the use of Rincon Valley. Rough
and crooked is made smooth and straight; safe
bridge and easy grade, a modern highway follows up the valley, with a brave firefly twinkling by night, to join the great National Trail

at Engle Dam. This is what they dreamed amid sand and thorn—and their dreams have all come true. Now who can say which was better, the hoping or the having?

It was pleasant enough, at least, on this day of hoping. Stargazer shuffled by farm and farm, and turned aside at last to where, with ax and pick and team and tackle, a big man was grubbing up mesquite roots. Unheeded, for the big man wrought sturdily, Charlie rode close; elbow on saddlehorn, chin on hand, he watched the work with mingled interest and pity.

"There," he said, and shuddered—"there, but for the grace of God, goes Charlie See!"

The big man straightened up and held a hand to his aching back. His face was brown and his hair was red, his eyes were big and blue and merry, and his big, homely, honest mouth was one broad grin.

"Why, if it ain't Nubbins! Welcome, little stranger! Hunting saddle horses—again?"

"Why, no, Big Boy—I'm not. Not this time."

Big Boy rubbed the bridge of his nose, dis-

concerted. "You always was before. Not
horses? Well, well! What say we go a-
visitin', then?" He squinted at the low sun.
"I'll call this a day, and we'll mosey right
home to my little old shack, and wolf down
a few eggs and such. Then we'll wash our
hands and faces right good, catch us up some
fresh horses out of the pasture, and terrapin
up the road a stretch. Bully big moonlight
night." He began unhooking his team.

"Fine! I just love to ride. Only came
about fifty miles to-day, too."

"I was thinkin' some of droppin' in on old
man Fenderson. I ain't been over there since
last night. Coalie! You, Zip! Ged-dap!"

"Mr. Adam Forbes," said Charlie, "I've got
you by the foot!"

"Now if you was wishful of any relaxa-
tions," said Adam after supper, "you might
side me up in the feet hills to-morrow, prospectin'."

"I might," said Charlie; "and then again I
mightn't. Don't you go and bet on it."

Adam stropped his razor. "You know

there's three cañons headin' off from Mac-
Cleod's Tank Park? And the farthest one,
that big, steep, rough, wide, long, high, ugly,
sandy, deep gash that runs anti-gogglin' north,
splittin' off these spindlin' little hills from the
main Caballo and Big Timber Mountain—
ever been through that? 'Pache Cañon, we
call it—though we got no license to."

"Part way," said Charlie. Then his voice
lit up with animation. "Say, Big Chump,
that's it! Them warty little hills here—that's
what makes us look down on you folks the way
we do. And here I thought all along it was
because you was splay-foot farmers, and un-
fortunate, you know, that way like all nesters
is. But blamed if I don't think it was them
hills, all the time. We got regular old he-
mountains, we have. But these here little old
squatty hills clutterin' up your back yard—
why, Adam, they ain't respectable, them hills
ain't—squanderin' round where a body might
stub his toe on 'em, any time. You ought
to pile 'em up, Adam. They look plumb
shiftless."

"That listens real good to me. You got

more brains than people say." Adam scraped tranquilly at cheek and chin, necessitating an occasional pause in his speech. "Now you can see for yourself how plumb foolish and futile a little runt of a man seems to a people that ain't never been stunted."

"'Seems' is a right good word," said Charlie. He blew out a smoke ring. "You sure picked the very word you wanted, that time. I didn't think you had sense enough."

Adam passed an appraising finger tip over his brown cheek; he stirred up fresh lather.

"Yes," he said musingly, "a little sawed off sliver like you sure does look right comical to a full-grown man. Like me. Or Hob Lull." He paused, brush in air, to regard his guest benignantly. "I wonder if girls feel that way too? Miss Lyn Dyer, now? Lull, he hangs round there right smart—and he's a fine, big, upstanding man." He lathered his face and rubbed it in. "First off, I fixed to assassinate him quiet, from behind. You know them two girls don't hardly know where they do live— always together, Harkey's house or Fenderson's. So I mistrusted, natural enough, that 'twas Miss Edith he was waitin' on. But I was mistook. Just in time to save his life from my bloody and brutal designs he began tolling Miss Lyn to one side to look at sunsets and books and such, givin' me a chance to buzz Miss Edith alone. Good thing for him. That's why I'm lettin' you tag along to-night —you can entertain Pete Harkey and Ma Fenderson and the old man, so's they won't pester me and Hobby."

"Like fun I will! If you fellows had any decent feeling at all you'd both of you clear out and give me a chance."

"Now, deary, you hadn't ought to talk like that—indeed you hadn't!" protested Adam. "You plumb distress me. You ought to declare yourself, feller. I'd always hate it if I was to slay you, and then find out I'd been meddlin' with Hobby Lull's private affairs. I'd hate that—I sure would!"

"Well now, there's no use of your askin' me for advice." Charlie's eyebrows shrugged, and so did his shoulders. "You'll have to decide these things for yourself. Say, you mangy, moth-eaten, slab-sided, long, lousy, lop-eared parallelopipedon, are you goin' to be all night dollin' up? Let's ride!"

"Don't blame you for bein' impatient. Hob, he's there now." Face and voice expressed fine tolerance; Adam looked into a scrap of broken mirror for careful knotting of a gay necktie.

"I won't be sorry to see Hob once more, at that," observed Charlie. "Always liked Lull. Took to him first time I ever saw him. That was seven years ago, when I was only a kid."

"Only a kid! Only—Great Cæsar's ghost, what are you now?"

"I'm twenty-five years old in my stocking feet. And here's how I met up with Lull. El Paso had a big ball game on with Silver City, and Hob, he wanted to be umpire. Nobody on either team would hear of it, and not one of the fifteen hundred rip-roarin', howlin' fans. It was sure a mean mess while it lasted. You see, there was a lot of money up on the game."

"And who umpired?"

"Hob."

IV

"Money was so scarce in that country that the babies had to cut their teeth on certified checks."

—Bluebeard for Happiness.

"The cauldrified and chittering truth."

—THE ETTRICK SHEPHERD.

"AS I was a-tellin' you, when I got switched off," said Adam, in the starlit road, "I found gold dust in 'Pache Cañon nigh onto a year ago. Not much—just a color—but it set me to thinkin'."

"How queer!" said Charlie.

"Yes, ain't it? You see, a long time ago, when the 'Paches were thick about here, they used to bring in gold to sell—coarse gold, big as rice, nearly. Never would tell where they got it; but when they wanted anything right bad they was right there with the stuff; coarse gold. All sorts of men tried all sorts of ways to find out where it came from. No go."

"Indians are mighty curious about gold," said Charlie. "Over in the Fort Stanton country, the Mescaleros used to bring in gold that same way—only it was fine gold, there. Along about 1880, Llewellyn, he was the agent; and Steve Utter, chief of police; and

82

Dave Easton, he was chief clerk; and Dave Pelman and Dave Sutherland—three Daves—and old Pat Coghlan—them six, they yammered away at one old buck till at last he agreed to show them. He was to get a four-horse team, harness and wagon, and his pick of stuff from the commissary to load up the wagon with. They was to go by night, and no other Indian was ever to know who told 'em, before or after—though how he proposed to account for that wagonload of plunder I don't know. I'll say he was a short-sighted Injun, anyway.

"Well, they started from the agency soon after midnight. They had to go downstream about a quarter, round a fishhook bend, on account of a mess of wire fence; and then they turned up through a *ciénaga* on a corduroy road, sort of a lane cut straight through the swamp, with the *tules*—cat-tail flags, you know —eight or ten feet high on each side. They was going single file, mighty quiet, Mister Mescalero-man in the lead. They heard just a little faint stir in the *tules,* and a sound like bees humming. Mister Redskin he keels over, shot full of arrows.   Not one leaf moving in the *tules;* all mighty still; they could hear the Injun pumping up blood, glug—glug—glug!   The white men went back home pretty punctual.   Come daylight they go back, police and everything.   There lays their guide with nine arrows through his midst.   And that was the end of him.

"But that wasn't the end of the gobbling gold.   Fifteen years after, Pat Coghlan and Dave Sutherland—the others having passed on or away, up, down, across or between—they throwed in with a lad called Durbin or something, and between them they honey-swoggled an old Mescalero named Falling Pine, and led him astray.   It took nigh two months, but they made a fetch of it.   Old Falling Pine, he allowed to lead 'em to the gold.

"Now as the years passed slowly by, Lorena, the Mescaleros had got quite some civilized; this old rooster, he held out for two thousand plunks, half in his grimy clutch, half on delivery.   He got it.   And they left Tularosa, eighteen miles below the agency, and ten miles

off the reservation, about nine o'clock of a fine
Saturday night.

"Well, sir, four miles above Tularosa the
wagon road drops off the mesa down to a little
swale between a sandstone cliff and Tularosa
Creek. They turned a corner, and there was
nine big bucks, wrapped up in blankets, heads
and all! There wasn't no arrows, and there
wasn't nothing said. Not a word. Those
nine bucks moved up beside Falling Pine, real
slow, one at a time. Each one leaned close,
pulled up a flap of the blanket, and looked old
Falling Pine in the eye, nose to nose. Then
he wrapped his blanket back over his face and
faded away. That was all.

"It was a great plenty. The plot thinned
right there. Falling Pine, he handed back
that thousand dollars advance money, like it
was hot, and he beat it for Tularosa. They
wanted him to try again, to tell 'em where the
stuff was, anyhow; they doubled the price on
him. He said no—not—*nunca*—nixy—*neinte*
—he guessed not—*nada*—not much—never!
He added that he was going to lead a better

life from then on, and wouldn't they please hush? And what I say unto you is this: How did them Indians know—hey?"

"Don't ask me," said Adam. "I've heard your story before, Charles—only your dead Injun had thirty-five arrows for souvenirs, 'stead of nine. The big idea was, of course, that where gold is found the white man comes along, and the Indian he has to move. But all this is neither here nor there, especially here, though heaven only knows what might have been under happier circumstances not under our control, as perhaps it was, though we are all liable to make mistakes in the best regulated families; yet perhaps I could find it in my heart to wish it were not otherwise, as the case may be."

"Nine arrows!" said Charlie firmly.

"Young fellow!" said Adam severely. "Be I telling this story or be I not? I been tryin' to relate about this may-be-so gold of mine, ever since you come—and dad burn it, you cut me off every time. I do wish you'd hush! Listen now! Of course there's placer gold all round Hillsboro; most anywheres west of

the river, for that matter.   But it's all fine dust
—never coarse gold beyond the river—and it
runs so seldom to the ton that no Injun would
ever get it.   So, thinks I, why not look in at
Apache Cañon?   It's the plumb lonesomest
place I know, and I don't believe anybody ever
had the heart to prospect it good.   So I went
up to Worden's and worked up from the lower
end.

"That was last year, and I have been prog-
nosticatin' round, off and on, ever since,
whenever I could get away from my farmin'.
I found a trace, mostly.   You can always get
a color round here, and no one place better
than another.   But when the rains begun this
year, so I could find water to pan with, I tried
it again, higher up.   And in a little flat side
draw, leadin' from between two miserable little
snubby hills off all alone, too low to send much
flood water down—there I begun to find float,
plumb promisin'.   I started to follow it up.
You know how—pan to right and left till the
stuff fails to show, mark the edge of the pay
dirt, go on up the hill and do the like again.
If the gold you're followin' has been carried

down by water the streak gets narrower as you go up a hillside, and pay dirt gets richer as it gets narrower. If the hill has been tossed about by the hell fires down below, all bets is off and no rule works, not even the exceptions. That's why they say gold is where you find it. But any time you find a fan-shaped strip of color on a hill that looks like it might have stayed put, or nearly so, it's worth while to follow it up. If you find the apex of that triangle you're apt to strike a pocket that will land you right side up with the great and good. Sometimes the apex has done been washed away; these water courses have run quite elsewhere other times. Oh, quite! But there's always a chance. Follow up a narrowing color and quit one that squanders round casual. Them's the rules.

"Well, sir, my pay dirt took to the side of that least hill, and she was shaping right smart like a triangle. Then my water give out. I was usin' a little tank in the rocks—no other without packing from MacCleod's Tank, five mile. And I had to get in my last cuttin' of alfalfa—pesky stuff! I cached my outfit and came on home.

"So there you are. It's been rainin' again; and I'm goin' out and try another whirl to-morrow, hit or miss. Go snooks with you if you're a mind to side me. What say?"

"Why, Big Chump, you're not such a bad old hoss thief, are you? Well, I thank you just as much, and I sure hope you'll make a ten-strike and everything like that; but, you see, I'm busy. Tell you what, Adam—you get Hob to go along, and I'll think about it."

"Oh, well, maybe it's a false alarm anyway," said Adam lightly. "I've known better things to fizzle. I get my fun, whatever happens. I can't stay cooped up on that measly old farm all the time. I need a little fresh air every so often. I'm a lot like Thompson's colt, that swum the river to get a drink."

"Don't like farmin', eh?"

"Why, yes, I do. Beats hellin' round, same as a stack of hay beats a stack of chips. They're right nice people here, Charlie, mighty pleasant and friendly and plumb cheer-

ful about the good time coming. And every
last one of 'em is here because this is the very
place he wants to be, and not because he happened to be here and didn't know how to get
away. That makes a power of difference.
They're plumb animated, these folks; if so be
they ain't just satisfied any place, they rise up
and depart. So we have no grand old
grouches. All the same, I'm free to admit
that I haven't quite the elbowroom I need."

"I know just how you feel," said Charlie;
"I've leased a township and fenced it in.
That's why I'm not at some round-up; all my
bossies right at home. And dog-gone if I
don't feel like I was in jail. But you people
can't be making much real money, Adam—
hauling over such roads as these. It is forty
miles from place to place, in here, while out
in the open it is only thirty or maybe twenty-
five. That's on account of the sand and the
curly places. And then you have nothing to
do in the wintertime."

"Well, now, it ain't so bad as you'd think—
not near. We raise plenty eggs, chickens,
pork and such truck, and fruit and vegetables.

Lots of milk and butter, too; not like when we didn't have anything but cows. Some of us have our little bunch of cattle in the foothills yet, and fat the steers on alfalfa, and get money for 'em when we sell. But that won't last long, I reckon. We're beginning to grow hogs on alfalfa and fat 'em on corn, smoke 'em and salt 'em and cross 'em with T and ship 'em to El Paso. I judge that ham, bacon and pork will be the main crops presently.

"Then we hurled up a grist mill since you was here, coöperative. Hob, he got up that. And we got a good wagon road through the mountain, to Upham. Goes up Redgate and out by MacCleod's Tank. Steepish, but no sand; when we get a car of stuff to ship we can haul twice as much as we can take to Rincon. We can't buy nothing at Upham, sure enough, and sometimes have to wait for our cars. But we can have stuff shipped to Upham from El Paso, and it's downhill coming back. Also, Hobby allows this Upham project will ably assist Rincon to wake up and build us a road up the valley."

"Hobby invented this wagon road, did he?"

"Every bit. We all chipped in to do the work. But Hob furnished the idea. That ain't all, either. From now on, we're going to have plenty to do, wintertimes. Mr. See, we got a factory up and ready to start. Yessir!"

"Easy, Big Chump! You'll strain yourself."

"Straight goods—no joking."

"Must be a hell of a factory!"

"She's all right, son. A home-grown factory. You go look at her to-morrow. Broom factory. Yessir! Every man jack of us raised a patch of broom corn. We sell it to ourselves or buy it of ourselves, whichever way you like it best; and anybody that wants to make brooms does that little thing. We ship from Upham and divvy up surplus. Every dollar's worth of broom corn draws down one dollar's share of the net profit, and every dollar's worth of labor does just that—no more, no less. It works out—with good faith and fair play."

"Hob?" said Johnny.

"That's the man." Adam Forbes let his

hand rest for a moment on the younger man's shoulder. "Charlie, you and me are all right in our place—but there ain't goin' to be no such place much longer. I reckon we ain't keepin' up with the times. So now you know why I wanted you should go prospectin' with me. Birds of a feather gather no moss."

"I judge maybe you're right. We both of us favor Thompson's colt, and that's a fact. Well, I am glad old Hob is making good. We had as good a chance as he did, only he had more sense."

"Always did," said Forbes heartily. "But he ain't makin' no big sight of money, if that's what you mean. Just making good. He's not working for Hob Lull especially. He's working for all hands and the cook. Hob always tries to get us to work together, like on a *'cequia*. There's other things—a heap of 'em. We've bought a community threshing machine. Hob has coaxed a lot of 'em into keeping bees. And he's ribbin' us up to try a cannin' factory in a year or two, for tomatoes and fruit. And a creamery, later. Hob is one long-headed

young people.   We aim to send him to represent for us sometime."

Charlie See laughed. "Gosh! I wish
you'd hurry up about it, then."

But there was no bitterness in his mirth.

V

"Never pray for rain on a rising barometer."
—*Naval Regulations.*

"Married men always make the worst husbands."
— *The Critic on the Hearth.*

"Although, contrary to his custom, he had a lady on his knee, he instructed the young prince in his royal duties."
—ANATOLE FRANCE.

LYN DYER lived with Uncle Dan in a little crowded house. Across the way stood a big lonesome house; there Edith Harkey lived with Daddy Pete.

Pete Harkey was a gentle, quiet and rather melancholy old man; Dan Fenderson was a fat, jolly and noisy youth of fifty. In relating other circumstances within the knowledge of the Border it would have been in no degree improper to have put the emphasis on the names of those two gentlemen. But this is "another story"; it is fitting that the youngsters take precedence; Lyn Dyer and Uncle Dan, Edith and her father.

Lyn Dyer—Carolyn, Lyn—had known no mother but Aunt Peg. The crowding of the little house was well performed by Lyn's three young cousins, Danjunior, Tomtom and Peggy.

The big house had been lonesome for ten years now. Edith's sisters and her one brother were all her seniors, all married, and all living within eye flight; two at Hillsboro, a scant twenty-five miles beyond the river—but the big house was not less lonesome for that.

The little crowded house and the big lonesome house were half way between Garfield post office and Derry. Both homes were in Sierra County, but they were barely across the boundary; the county line made the southern limit of each farm. This was no chance but a choosing, and that a pointed one; having to do with that other story of those two old men.

In Dona Ana County taxes were high and life was cheap. Since the Civil War, Dona Ana had been bedeviled by the rule of professional politicians. Sierra—aside from Lake Valley and Hillsboro—had very little ruling and needed less; commonly enough there was only one ticket for county officers, and that was picked by a volunteer committee from both parties. Sierra was an American county, and took pride that she had kept free from feuds and had no bandits within her borders. Not that Mexicans were such evildoers. But where there was an overwhelming Mexican vote there was a large purchasable vote; which meant that purchasers took office. Unjust administration followed—oppression, lawsuits and lawlessness, revenge, bloodshed, feuds, anarchy. Result: More expense, more taxes, more bribing, more bribers, more oppression to recoup the cost of officeholding. *Caveat pre-emptor*—let the homesteader beware!

That unhappy time is now past and done with.

"Lyn! Lyn! Edith! Do come here and see what Adam Forbes has brought in," grumbled Uncle Dan. "Another cowboy, and you just got rid of Tom Bourbonia. It does beat all!"

Mr. Fenderson, uttering the above complaint, stood on his porch in the light from his open door and struck hands with two men there; after which he slapped them violently on the back.

"Come in!" cried Lyn from the doorway. Her eyes were shining. She dropped a curtsy.

" 'Come in, come in—ye shall fare most kind!' "

"Don't you believe Uncle Dan," said Edith. "We tried every way to make Tommy stay over—didn't we, Lyn?"

The story is not able to give an exact record of the next minutes. Of the five young people —for Mr. Hobby Lull was there, as prophesied—of the five young people, five were talking at once; and Uncle Dan, above them all, boomed directions to Danjunior as to the horses of his visitors.

"Daniel! Stop that noise!" said Aunt Peg severely. "You boys come on in the house. Mr. Charlie, I'm glad to see you."

"Now, here!" protested Forbes. "Isn't anybody going to be glad to see me?"

"But, Adam, we can see you any time," explained Edith. "While Mr. See—"

"Her eyes went twinkle, twinkle, but her nose went 'Sniff! Sniff!' " said Adam dolefully. "Excuse me if I seem to interrupt."

"But Mr. See—"

"Charlie," said See.

"But Charlie makes himself a stranger.

We haven't seen you for six months, Mr. See."

"Charlie," said Mr. See again. "Six months and eight days."

Mr. Hobby Lull sighed dreamily. "Dear me! It doesn't seem over two weeks!"

A mesquite fire crackled in the friendly room. The night air bore no chill; it was the meaning of that fire to be cheerful; the wide old fireplace was the heart of the house. Adam Forbes spread his fingers to the blaze and sighed luxuriously.

"Charlie, when you build your house you want a fireplace like this in every room. Hob, who's going to sell Charlie a farm?"

"What's the matter with yours?"

Adam appeared a little disconcerted at this suggestion. "That idea hadn't struck me, exactly," he confessed. "But it may come to that yet. Lots of things may happen. I might find my placer gold, say. Didn't know I was fixing to find a gold mine, did you? Well, I am. I wanted Charlie to go snooks with me, but he hasn't got time. Me, I've been projectin' and pirootin' over the pinnacles after that gold for a year now, and I've just about got it tracked to its lair. To-morrow—"

"Oh, gold!" said Lyn disdainfully, and wrinkled her nose.

> *"Ain't I told you a hundred times—*
> *Baby!*
> *Ain't I told you a hundred times,*
> *There ain't no money in the placer mines?*
> *Baby!"*

"Lyn! Wherever do you pick up such de-plorable songs?" said Aunt Peg, highly scan-dalized. "But she's right, Adam. The best gold is like that in the old fable—buried under your apple trees. You dig there faithfully and you will need no placer mines."

White Edith turned to Charlie See.

"If you really intend to buy a farm here you ought to be getting about it. You might wait too long, Mr. See."

"Charlie. Exactly what do you mean by that remark, my fair-haired child?"

"Here! This has gone far enough!" de-clared Hob. "We men have got to stand to-gether—or else pull stakes and go where the women cease from troubling and the weary are at rest. Don't you let her threats get you rattled, Charlie See. We'll protect you."

"Silly! I meant, of course, that the Mexicans are not selling their lands cheaply now, as they used to do."

"Not so you could notice it," said Uncle Dan. "Those that wanted to sell, they've sold and gone, just about all of them. What few are left are the solid ones. Not half-bad neighbors either. Pretty good sort. They're apt to stick."

"Not long," said Hobby rather sadly. "They'll go, and we'll go too, most of us. The big dam will be built, some time or other; we'll be offered some real money. We'll grab it and drift. Strangers will take comfort where we've grubbed out stumps. We are the scene shifters. The play will take place later. 'Sall right; I hope the actors get a hand. But I hate to think of strangers living—well, in this old house. Say, we've had some happy times here."

"Won't you please hush?" said Adam. "Why so doleful? There's more happy times in stock. This bunch don't have to move away. Why, when I get my gold mine in action we can all live happy ever after. Tomorrow—"

"Hobby is right," said Aunt Peg. "Pick your words as you please, bad luck or improvidence on the one side, thrift or greed on the other—yes, and as many more words of praise or blame as you care for; and the fact remains that the people who care for other things more than they do for money are slowly crowded out by the people who care more for money than for anything else."

"Uncle Dan, is that why you grasping Scotchmen have crowded out the Irish round these parts?" inquired Charlie. "McClintock, MacCleod, Simpson, Forbes, Campbell, Monroe, Fenderson, Stewart, Buchanan—why, say, there's a raft of you here; and across the river it is worse."

"You touch there on a very singular thing, Mr. Charlie. Not that we crowded out the Irish. There were only a few families, and most of them are here yet. They happened to come first, and named the settlements—

that's all. But for the Scotch—you find more good Scots' names to the hundred, once you strike the hills, than you will find to the thousand on the plain country. Love of the hills is in the blood of them; they followed the Rocky Mountains down from Canada."

"But, Uncle Dan," said Hobby, "how did so many of them happen to be in Canada?"

"Scotland was a poor country and a cold country, England was rich and warm, Canada was cold and hard. The English had no call to Canada, the Hudson Bay Company captained their outflung posts with Scotchmen; the easier that the Hanoverian kings, as a matter of policy, harried the Jacobite clans by fair means and foul. You were speaking of across the river. That is another curious matter. The California Company, now—ruling a dozen dukedoms—California lends the name of it and supplied the money; but the heads that first dreamed it were four long Scottish heads. And their brand is the John Cross. Any stranger cowman would read that brand as J Half Circle Cross. But we call it John Cross. And why, sirs?"

"I'm sure I don't know," said Hobby. "It was always the John Cross and it never entered my head to ask why."

"Look you there, now!" Uncle Dan held out an open palm and traced on it with a stubby and triumphant finger. "Their fathers had served John Company, the Hudson Bay Company! And there you are linked back with two hundred years! 'John Company has a long arm,' they said; 'John Company lost a good man there!' How the name began is beyond my sure knowing; but it is in my mind that it goes back farther still, to the East India Company, to Clive and to Madras. Lyn, you are the bookman, I'll get you to look it up some of these—Lyn! Lyn! Charlie See! The young devils! Now wouldn't that jar you?"

"A fool and his honey are soon started," observed Adam.

"We're out here, Uncle Dan; all nice and comfy. There's a moon. And itty-bitsy stars," answered a soothing voice—Charlie See's—from the porch. "Oodles of stars. How I wonder what they are. G'wan, Uncle

Dan—tell us about the East India Company now."

Hobby Lull rose tragically and bestowed a withering glance upon Uncle Dan. "You old fat fallacy with an undistributed middle—see what you've done now! You and your John Company! Go to bed! Forbes, you brought this man See.   You go home!"

"Overlook it this one time," urged Forbes. "Don't send us away—the girls are going to sing.   Forgive us all both, and I'll get rid of See to-morrow."

"Be sure you do, then.   Lyn!   Come here to me."

"Don't shoot, colonel, I'll come down," said Lyn.

Her small face was downcast and demure. Charlie See came tiptoe after her and sidled furtively to the fire.

"Sing, then," commanded Hobby.   He brought the guitars and gave one to each girl.

The coals glowed on the hearth; side by side, the fair head and the brown bent at the task of tuning.   That laughing circle was

scattered long ago and it was written that
never again should all those friendly faces
gather by any hearthfire—never again. It
has happened so many, many times; even to
you and to me, so many, many times! But we
learn nothing; we are still bitter, and hard,
and unkind—with kindness so cheap and so
priceless—as if there was no such thing as
loss or change or death.

And because of some hours of your own,
it is hoped you will not smile at the songs of
that lost happy hour. They were old-fashioned songs; indeed, it is feared they might almost be called Victorian. Their bourgeois
simplicity carried no suggestive double meaning.

"When other lips and other hearts"—that
was what they sang, brown Lyn and white
Edith. Kirkconnel Lea they sang, and Jeanie
Morrison, and Rosamond:

> *Rose o' the world, what man would wed*
> *When he might dream of your face instead?*

Folly? Perhaps. Perhaps, too, in a world
where we can but love and where we must

lose, it may be no unwisdom if only love and loss seem worth the singing.

The swift hour passed.   The last song, even as the first, was poignant with the happy sadness of youth:

> *When my heart is sad and troubled,*
>   *Then my quivering lips shall say,*
> *"Oh! by and by you will forget me,*
>   *By and by when far away!"*

Good-bys were said at last; Forbes and See put foot to stirrup and rode jingling into the white moonlight; the others stood silent on the porch and watched them go.   A hundred yards down the road, Adam Forbes drew rein. A guitar throbbed low behind them.

"Hark," he said.

Edith Harkey stood in the shaft of golden light from the doorway; she bore herself like the Winged Victory; her voice thrilled across the quiet of the moonlit night:

> *"Never the nightingale,*
>   *Oh, my dear!*
> *Never again the lark*
>   *Thou wilt hear;*
> *Though dusk and the morning still*

Tap at thy window-sill,
Though ever love call and call
Thou wilt not hear at all,
*   My dear, my dear!"*

The sad notes melted into the sweet pagan heartbreak of the enchanted night. They turned to go.

"A fine girl," said Adam Forbes. "The only girl! To-morrow—"

He fell silent; again in his heart that parting cadence knelled with keen and intolerable sorrow. The roots of his hair prickled, ants crawled on his spine. So tingles the pulsing blood, perhaps, when a man is fey, when the kisses of his mouth are numbered.

Edith went home to the big lonely house, but Lyn Dyer and Hobby Lull lingered by the low fire. Mr. Lull assumed a dignified pose before the fireplace, feet well apart and his hands clasped behind his back. He regarded Miss Dyer with a twinkling eye.

"Have you anything to say to the court before sentence is pronounced?" he inquired with lofty judicial calm.

Miss Dyer avoided his glance. She stood

drooping before him; she looked to one side at the floor; she looked to the other side at the floor. The toe of her little shoe poked and twisted at a knot in the floor.

"Extenuating circumstances?" she suggested hopefully.

"Name them to the court."

"The—the moon, I guess." The inquisitive shoe traced crosses and circles upon the knot in the flooring. "And Charlie See," she added desperately. "Charlie has such eloquent eyes, Hobby—don't you think?"

She raised her little curly head for a tentative peep at the court; her own eyes were shining with mischief. The court unclasped its hands.

"I ought to shake you," declared Hobby. But he did not shake her at all.

"You're the only young man in Garfield who wears his face clean-shaven," remarked Lyn reflectively, a little later. "Charlie would look much better without a mustache, I think."

He pushed her away and tipped up her chin with a gentle hand so that he could look into her eyes. "Little brown lady with curly eyes and laughing hair—are you quite fair to Charlie See?"

"No," said Lyn contritely, "I'm not. I suppose we ought to tell him."

"We ought to tell everybody. So far as I am concerned, I would enjoy being a sandwich man placarded in big letters: 'Property of Miss Lyn Dyer.'"

"Why, Hobbiest—I thought it was rather nice that we had such a great big secret all our own. But you're right—I see that now. I should have met him at the door, I suppose, and said, 'You are merely wasting your time, Mr. See. I will never desert my Wilkins!' Only that might have been a little awkward, in a way, because, you see, 'Nobody asked you to,' he said—or might have said."

"He never told you, then?"

"Not a word."

"But you knew?"

"Yes," said Lyn. "I knew." She twisted a button on his coat and spoke with a little wistful catch in her voice. "I do like him,

Hobby—I can't help it. Only so much."
She indicated how much on the nail of a small
finger. "Just a little teeny bit. But that
little bit is—"

"Strictly plutonic?"

"Yes," she said, in a small meek voice.
"How did you know? He makes me like
him, Hobbiest. It—it scares me sometimes."

"Pretty cool, I'll say, for a girl that has
only been engaged a week, if you should happen to ask me."

"Oh, but that's not the same thing—not the
same thing at all! You couldn't keep me
from liking you, not if you tried ever so hard.
That is all settled. But Charlie makes me
like him. You see, he is such a real people; I feel like the Griffin did about the
Minor Canon: 'He was brave and good and
honest, and I think I should have relished
him.' "

Hobby held her at arm's length and regarded her quizzically. "So young, and yet
so tender?"

" 'So young, my lord, and true.' "

"Well," said Hobby resignedly, "I suppose

we'll have to quarrel, of course.   They all do.
But I don't know how to go about it.   What
do I say next?"

"I might as well tell you the worst, angelest
pieface.   You ought to know what a shocking
horrid little creature your brown girl really
is.   You won't ever tell—honest-to-goodness,
cross-your-heart-and-hope-to-die?"

"Never."

"Say it, then."

"Honest-to-goodness, cross-my-heart-and-
hope-to-die."

She buried her face on his breast.   "I
dreamed about him last night, Hobby.
Wasn't that queer?   I hadn't thought of him
before for months—weeks, anyhow."

"A week, maybe?" suggested Hobby.

"Oh, more than that!   Two weeks, at the
very least.   I—I hate to tell you," she whispered.   "I—I dreamed I liked him almost as
much as I do you!"

"Why, you brazen little bigamist!"

"Yes, I am—I mean, ain't I?" she assented
complacently, for his arms belied his words.
"But that's not the worst, Hobbiest—that's not

nearly the dreadfulest.   When I woke up I—
I wrote some—some verses about my dream.
Are you awfully angry?   We'll burn them to-
gether after you read them."

"Woman, produce those verses!   I will take
charge of them as 'Exhibit A.' "

"And then you'll beat me, please?"

"Oh, no," said Hobby magnanimously.
"That's nothing!   Pish, tush!   Why, Lino-
leum, I feel that way about lots of girls.
Molly Sullivan, now—"

"Hobby!"

"I always like to dream of Molly.   One of
the best companions to take along in a
dream—"

"Only-est!   Please don't!"

"Well, then," said Hobby, "I won't—on one
condition.   It is to be distinctly understood
under no circumstances are you ever to call
me Charlie.   I won't stand for it.   Dig up
your accursed doggerel!"

This is what Hobby Lull read aloud, with
exaggerated fervor, while Lyn huddled by the
dying fire and hid her burning face in her
hands:

Last night I kissed you as you slept,
  For all night long I dreamed of you;
Lower and low the hearth fire crept,
  The embers glowed and dimmed; we two
Heard the wind rave at bolt and door
  With all the world shut out and fast,
Doubted, hoped, questioned, feared no more,
  And all we sought was ours at last.

I do not love you, dear. I never loved you,
  Grudged what I gave, a wayward tenderness;
Yet in my dream I wooed you with white arms
  And lingering soft caress.
Now for all years to come I must remember,
  When fires burn dim and low,
This false dear dream of mine, that stolen hour—
  Your face of long ago.

I shall awaken in some midnight lonely,
  I shall remember you as one apart,
How for one hour of dream I loved you only
  And held you in my heart.
And you, through all the years since first you met me
  Still let my memory gleam;
Oh, my old lover! Do not quite forget me!
  I loved you—in my dream!

Hobby cleared his throat impressively,

tapped his table with the paper, and assumed measured judicial accents.

"This incriminating document proves—hah —hum—"

"To the satisfaction of the court," prompted Lyn in a muffled voice.

"To the satisfaction of the court—I thank you! To the very great satisfaction of the court, this document, together with the bare-faced manner in which you have brought this evidence to the cognizance of this court—it proves, little Lady Lyn, that you are compact all of loyalty and clean honor—and the sentence of this court is, Imprisonment for life!"

He held out his arms, and the culprit crept gladly to prison.

VI

"Then there was a star danc'd, and under that was I born."
—*Much Ado About Nothing.*

COLE RALSTON rose up in a red windy dawn; he cupped his hands to his mouth and called out lustily: "Beds!"

All around, men roused up in the half darkness and took up the word, laughing, as they dressed: "Beds!   Beds!"

The call meant that the wagon was to be moved to-day; that each man was to roll bedding and tarp to a hard and tight-roped cylinder, and was then to carry it to a stack by the bed wagon.

The cook bent over pots and pans, an active demon by a wind-blown fire; here already the bobtail ate their private breakfast, that they might depart in haste to relieve the last guard —now slowly moving the herd from the bed ground, half a mile away.

Cole moved over where Johnny Dines was making up his bed roll.

"Needn't hurry with that bed, Johnny," he

116

said in an undertone. "You move the wagon to Preisser Lake this mornin'. Besides, you may want to hold something out of your bed. You're to slip away after dinner and edge over towards Hillsboro. Help Hiram bring his cattle back when he gets ready. Tell him we'll be round Aleman all this week, so he might better come back through MacCleod's Pass. I don't know within fifty mile where the John Cross wagon is."

Johnny nodded, abandoning his bed making. *"Bueno, señor!"* He took a pair of leather chaparejos from the bed, regarded them doubtfully and threw them back.

"Guess I won't take the chaps. Don't need them much except on the river work, in the mesquite; and they're so cussed, all-fired hot."

"Say, John, you won't need your mount, I reckon. Just take one horse. Lot of our runaway horses in the John Cross pasture. You can ride them—and take your pick for your mount when you come back. That's all. Road from Upham goes straight west through the mountains. Once you pass the summit you see your own country."

"Got you," said Johnny.

He went hotfoot to the wagon, grabbed a tin washbasin, held it under the water-barrel faucet and made a spluttering toilet—first man, since he had not rolled his bed.

The bobtail rode off at a laughing gallop. Daylight grew. The horse herd drew near with a soft drumming of trotting feet in the sand. Johnny rustled tools from the stacked tin plates and cups; he stabbed a mighty beefsteak with his iron fork; he added hot sourdough biscuit, a big spoonful of hot canned corn; he poured himself a cup of hot black coffee, sat down on one of his own feet in the sand, and became a busy man.

Others joined that business. The last guard came in; the chattering circle round the fire grew with surprising swiftness. Each, as he finished, carried cup, plate and iron cutlery to the huge dishpan by the chuck box, turned his night horse loose, and strode off to the horse herd, making a noose in his rope. They made a circle round the big horse herd, a rope from each to each by way of a corral on three sides of it; night wrangler and day

wrangler, mounted, holding down the fourth
side. Grumbling dayherders caught their
horses, saddled with miraculous swiftness and
departed to take over the herd. The bobtail
was back before the roping out of horses was
completed. While the bobtail roped out their
horses, Johnny and the two wranglers lured
out the four big brown mules for the chuck
wagon and the two small brown mules for the
bed wagon, tied them to convenient soapweeds
and hung a nose bag full of corn on each
willing brown head. Last of all the horse
wrangler caught his horse. The night wrangler was to ride the bed wagon, so he needed
no horse.

The circle of men melted away from about
the horse herd; there was a swift saddling,
with occasional tumult of a bucking rebel; the
horse herd grazed quietly away; the wranglers
went to breakfast; even as they squatted cross-
legged by the fire the last horse was saddled,
the Bar Cross outfit was off to eastward to begin the day's drive, half a dozen horses pitching enthusiastically, cheered by ironical encouragement and advice bestowed on their

riders. The sun would not be up for half an hour yet. Forty men had dressed, rolled their beds, eaten, roped out their day's horses in the half light from a dodging mob of four hundred head, saddled and started. Fifty minutes had passed since the first call of beds. The day herd was a mile away, grazing down the long road to Preisser Lake; at the chuck box the cook made a prodigious clatter of dish washing.

The Bar Cross had shipped the north drive of steers from Engle; the wagon had then wandered southward for sixty miles to Fort Selden, there to begin the south work in a series of long zigzags across the broad plain. This was the morrow after that day on which Charlie See had ridden to Garfield.

The wagon was halfway home to Engle now; camped on the central run-off of the desert drainage system, at the northmost of the chain of shallow wet-weather lakes— known as Red Lakes—lying east and south from Point of Rocks Hills. Elsewhere these had been considerable hills; ten or fifteen miles square of steepish sugar loaves, semi-independent, with wide straits of grassy plain winding between; but here, dumped down in the center of the plain, they seemed pathetically insignificant and paltry against the background of mighty hill, Timber Mountain black in the west, San Andreas gleaming monstrous against the rising sun.

Theoretically, the Jornada was fifty miles wide here; in reality it was much wider; in seeming it was twice as wide. From Red Lakes as a center you looked up an interminable dazzle of slope to the San Andreas, up and up over a broken bench country to Timber Mountain, the black base of it high above the level of Point o' Rocks at its highest summit; and toward the north looked up and up and up again along a smoother and gentler slope ending in a blank nothingness, against which the eye strained vainly.

Johnny sipped another cup of coffee with the wranglers; he smoked a cigarette; he put on fresh clothing from his bed; he took his gun from his bed and buckled the belt loosely at his waist. His toilet completed, he rolled his bed. By this time the wranglers had breakfasted.

They piled the bed rolls high on the bed wagon and roped them tight for safe riding; they harnessed and hitched the two small mules. The night wrangler tied the reins to the dashboard and climbed to the top of the stacked bedding.

"You see that these mules get started, will you, Pat? I'm going to sleep. They'll tag along after the chuck wagon if you'll start 'em once," said the night wrangler. Discipline did not allow the night wrangler a name. He stretched out luxuriously, his broad hat over his face.

Johnny and Pat—Pat was the horse wrangler—hitched the four mules to the chuck wagon, after which Pat rounded up his scattered charges and drove them down to the lake for water.

All this time the red-head cook had been stowing away his housekeeping, exactly three times as fast as you would expect three men to do it. A good cook, a clean cook, swiftest of

all cooks, Enriquez—also despot and holy
terror as a side line.   Henry was the human
hangnail.   It is a curious thing that all round-
up cooks are cranks; a fact which favors reflection.   If it be found that cooking and ferocity
stand in the relation of cause to effect, a new
light is thrown on an old question.

The last Dutch oven was stowed away, the
lid of the chuck box snapped shut and locked.
Johnny tossed the few remaining beds up to
the cook.

"Do we fill the barrel here, Henry?"

"No.   Dees water muddy.   Preisser Lake
she am deep and clean.   De company ees buil'
a dam dere, yes.   Han' me dees lines.   You
Mag! Jake!   Rattle yo' hocks!"

With creaking of harness and groaning of
axle, the chuck wagon led off on a grass-grown
road winding away to the northwest, a faint
track used only by the round-up; travel
kept to the old Santa Fé trail, to the
west, beyond the railroad.   Johnny started
the other team.   Unguided, the bed wagon
jounced and bumped over grassy hummocks
until it reached the old road and turned

in contentedly at the tail of the chuck wagon. The sleeping wrangler mumbled, rolled precariously on his high lurching bed, and settled back to sleep.

Johnny laughed and rode ahead to help Pat. They drove the horses in a wide detour round the slow-grazing day herd. But the chuck wagon held the right of way over everything; when it came to pass the herd an hour or two later, it would be for the herd to swerve aside.

The sun was high and hot now; Preisser Hill, a thin long shadow, rose dim above the plain; Upham tower and tank loomed high and spectral, ahead and at the left.

"How do I get from Upham to the river, Pat? I'm new to this country."

"Wagon road due west to MacCleod's Pass."

"Can't see any pass from here."

"Naw. You slip into fold between the hills, and twist round like a figure three. Then you come to a big open park and MacCleod's Tank. Three draws run down from the park to the river. 'Pache cañon, the biggest, runs north to nowhere; Redgate, on the left, twists round to Garfield. Wagon road goes down Redgate. And Deadman Draw, in between, bears due west and heap down, short and sweet. Riding?"

"Yep. Hillsboro. The middle draw will be the one for me, then."

By ten o'clock they watered the horse herd at Preisser Lake; the wagons toiled far behind. Half a mile away they picked the camp site, with a little ridge for wind-break, soapweeds to tie night horses to, wood handy, and a near-by valley to be a bed ground for the herd; a valley wide, open, free from brush, gully or dog holes.

They dragged up a great pile of mesquite roots and built a fire; Pat went to watch his horses and Johnny returned to the lake. Henry drove the wagon into the lake, hub deep; Johnny stood on the hub and dipped buckets of water, which he handed up for the cook to pour into the barrel.

While these two filled the barrel the grumbling night wrangler drove on to the fire; when the slow chuck wagon trundled up, the night-hawk had unharnessed his span of mules, spread his roll in the cool shade under the bed wagon, and was already asleep. The cook tossed down the odd beds, handed down to Johnny certain pots, pans, ovens; he jumped down—slap, snap, clatter, flash!—the ovens were on the fire, the chuck box open, flour in the bread pan; Henry was at his profession, mixing bread on the table made by the open lid of the chuck box, upheld by a hinged leg which fell into place as the lid tilted down.

Johnny unharnessed; he unrolled a tarp which wrapped a quarter of beef, and hung the beef on the big brake; he filled the ten-gallon coffee kettle and took it to the fire.

"Henry," he said cautiously, "can you let me have some cold bread and meat—enough for night and morning? I'm for Hillsboro. Goin' to make a dry camp beyond the river somewhere. Hillsboro's too far and Garfield not far enough. So I don't want to stay at the settlements to-night. I'll lay out and stake my horse, I reckon. Got to find the John Cross wagon to-morrow, and it'll take me all my time—so I don't want to wait for dinner."

"Humph!" With a single motion Henry flirted a shovelful of glowing coals from the fire; a second motion twisted a small meat oven into place over those coals. A big spoonful of lard followed. "Rustle a can and boil you some coffee. Open can tomatoes; pour 'em in a plate. Use can. Ground coffee in box— top shelf. I'll have bread done for you when coffee boils!"

While he spoke his hands were busy. He dragged from the chuck box a dishpan full of steaks, cut the night before. With a brisk slap he spread a mighty steak on the chuck box lid, sprinkled it with salt, swept it through the flour in his bread pan with precisely the wrist-twisting motion of a man stropping a razor, and spread the steak in the hissing lard.

"Cook you another bimeby for night," he grunted, and emptied his sour-dough sponge into the bread pan. A snappy cook, Henry; on occasion he had built dinner for thirty men in thirty minutes, by the watch, from the time the wagon stopped—bread, coffee, steak and fried potatoes—steak and potatoes made ready for cooking the night before, of course.

Henry had not known he was being timed, either; he was that kind of a cook.

Johnny gave thanks and ate; he rolled a substantial lunch in a clean flour sack and tied it in his slicker behind the saddle. He rode to the horse herd; Pat rounded up the horses and Johnny snared his Twilight horse for the trip. Twilight was a *grullo;* that is to say, he was precisely the color of a Maltese cat—a sleek velvet slaty-blue; a graceful, half-wild creature, dainty muzzled, clean legged as a deer. Pat held Twilight by bit and bridle and made soothing statements to him while Johnny saddled. Johnny slid into the saddle, there was a brief hair-stirring session of bucking; then Twilight sneezed cheerfully and set off on a businesslike trot. Johnny waved good-by, and turned across the gray plain toward Upham. Looking back, he saw the van of the day herd just showing up, a blur in the southeast.

Six miles brought him to Upham—side track, section house, low station, windmill tower and tank; there was a deep well here. He crossed the old white scar of the Santa Fé

trail, broad, deep worn, little used and half
forgotten. A new and narrow road turned
here at right angles to the old trail and led
ruler-straight to the west. Johnny followed
this climbing road, riding softly; bands of
cattle stirred uneasily and made off to left or
right in frantic run or shuffling trot. The
road curved once only, close to the hills, to
round the head of a rock-walled, deep, narrow
gash, square and straight and sheer, reaching
away toward Rincon, paralleling the course of
the mountains. No soft water-washed curves
marked that grim gash; here the earth crust
had cracked and fallen apart; for twenty miles
that gray crack made an impassable barrier;
between here and the bare low hills was a No
Man's Land.

Midway of the twisting pass Johnny came
to a gate in a drift fence strung from bluff to
bluff; here was a frontier of the Bar Cross
country. He passed the outpost hills and
came out to a rolling open park, a big square
corral of cedar pickets, an earthen dam, a
deep five-acre tank of water. About this tank
two or three hundred head of cattle basked

comfortably in the warm sun, most of them lying down. They were gentle cattle; Johnny rode slowly among them without stirring up excitement. "River cattle—nester cattle," said Johnny. There were many brands, few of which he had seen before, though he had heard of most of them.

A fresh bunch of cattle topped a riverward ridge; the leaders raised their heads, snorted, turned and fled; Twilight leaped in pursuit. "River cattle—*bosque* cattle—outlaws!" said Johnny. From the tail of his eye, as Twilight thundered across the valley, Johnny was aware of a deep gashed cañon heading in the north, of a notch in the western rim of the saucer-shaped basin, and a dark pass at the left. The cattle turned to the left. Johnny closed in on them, taking down his rope from the saddle horn. Twenty head—among them one Bar Cross cow with an unbranded calf some eight or ten months old. Johnny's noose whirled open, he drove the spurs home and plunged into a whistling wind. He drew close, he made his cast and missed it; Twilight swerved aside at the very instant of the throw, the rope dragged at his legs, he fell to frantic pitching. Johnny gathered up the rope, massaged his refractory mount with it, brought him to reason; in time to see a dust cloud of cattle drop into the leftward pass. Twilight flashed after. As they dived into the pass they came to the wagon road again.

"This is Redgate," thought Johnny.

They careened down the steep curves, the cattle were just ahead; Twilight swooped upon them, scattered the tailenders, drove ahead for the Bar Cross cow and her long-ear. A low saddleback pass appeared at the right, a winding trail led up to an overhanging promontory under the pass; below, the wagon road made a deep cut by the base of the hill. Distrusting the cut road as the work of man, the leaders took to the trail. Twilight was at their heels; at the crown of the little promontory Johnny threw again, and his rope circled the long-ear's neck. Johnny flipped the slack, the yearling crossed it and fell crashing; Johnny leaped off and ran down the rope, loosing the hogging string at his waist as he ran; he gathered the yearling's struggling feet and hog-tied them. Twilight looked on, panting but complacent.

"Look proud, now do, you ridiculous old fool!" said Johnny. "Ain't you never goin' to learn no sense a-tall? You old skeezicks! You've lost a shoe, too."

He coiled his rope and tied it to the saddle horn; from under the horn on the other side he took a running iron, held there by a slitted leather—an iron rod three-eighths of an inch in diameter, a foot long and shaped like a shepherd's crook. He gathered up dead branches of mahogany bush and made a small fire, cunningly built for a quick draft, close beside the yearling; he thrust the hook part of the branding iron into the hottest fire; and while it was heating he returned to give grave reprimand and instruction to Twilight. That culprit listened attentively, bright-eyed and watchful; managing in some way to bear himself so as to suggest a man who looks over the top of his spectacles while rubbing his chin with a thoughtful thumb. When the iron was hot Johnny proceeded to put the Bar Cross brand on the protesting yearling. Looking up, he became aware of a man riding soberly down the cañon toward him. Johnny waved his hand and shoved his iron into the fire for a second heating.

The newcomer rode up the trail and halted; a big red-headed man with a big square face and twinkling eyes. He fished for tobacco and rolled a cigarette.

"Thought I knew all the Bar Cross waddies. You haven't been wearin' the crop and split very long, have you?"

"They just heard of me lately," explained Johnny.

"I know that Twilight horse of yours. Saw him last spring at the round-up. Purty as a picture, ain't he?"

"Humph! Pretty is as pretty does." Johnny returned to his branding. "He made me miss my throw, and now I'm in the wrong cañon. I aimed to take the draw north of here, for Hillsboro."

The newcomer leaned on his saddle horn.

"Deadman? Well, you could cross over through this pass if you was right set on it. But it's a mean place on the far side—slick, smooth rock. You might as well go on by way of Garfield now. You won't lose but a mile or two, and you'll have fine company— me. Or—say, if you're going that way, why can't you mail a letter for me? Then I won't have to go at all. I'd be much obliged to you if you would. That was all I was going for, to mail some location notices."

"Sure I will. I kind of want to see Garfield anyhow. Never been there. Crop and split the right. So that's done. I'll keep this piece of ear for tally."

The other took a large envelope from his saddle pockets and handed it over. Dines stuck it in the bosom of his flannel shirt.

"I ain't got no stamps. This letter'll need two, I guess. Here's the nickel. Will you please kindly stick 'em on for me?"

"Sure," said Dines again. He undid the yearling's legs. "Now, young fellow, go find your mammy. Go a-snuffin'!"

The yearling scrambled to his feet, bellowing. Johnny jerked him round by the tail so that his nose pointed down the cañon; the newcomer jumped his horse and shook a stirrup

Courtesy Ruth Koerner Oliver

Bar Cross Man

and slapped his thigh with his hat; the yearling departed.

"Well, I'll be getting on back to camp,"
said the newcomer. "So long! Much obliged to you."

"So long!" said Johnny.

He waved his hand. The other waved
answer as he took the trail. He jogged in
leisurely fashion up the cañon. Dines paused
to tread out the remaining fire, took up his
branding iron by the cool end, and rode whistling down the cañon, swinging the iron to
cool it before he slipped it to its appointed
place below his saddle horn.

VII

"May God be merciful to him and to us all."
—*The Advocate of Arras.*

"**B**ETTER come along and share my guilty splendor," urged Adam Forbes, toe to stirrup.

Charlie See shook his head. "Not none. Here I rest. Gold is nothing to me. I've got no time for frivolity. I want but little here below and want that little now. Say, Adam —don't you never carry a gun?"

"Naw. I take a rifle, of course, for reindeer, snow dear, dear me and antelope—but I haven't packed a gun for two years. No need of it here. Well, if you won't side me, you won't. I'm sorry, but you see how it is about me going right now," said Adam, swinging into the saddle. "The water in that little tank of mine won't last long, and there may not be any more rains this fall. So long! You just make yourself at home."

"Good luck, Adam. And you might wish me the same. While you're gone, I may want to make a little journey from bad to worse."

Adam gathered up his lead rope. "Good luck, Charlie." But a troubled look came to his eyes as he passed through the gate; in his heart he thought his friend rode late and vainly from Selden Hill.

The pack horse jogged alongside, his friendly head at Adam's knee. It was earliest morning and they were still in the fresh cool shadow of the low eastern hills. Farther north the enormous bulk of Timber Mountain loomed monstrous in the sky, and there the shadows were deep and dense, impenetrably black; there night lingered visible, brighter that in all the wide arc to westward, benchland and mighty hill were drenched with sparkling sun.

Adam rode with a pleasant jingling of spurs. He passed through Garfield town, or town-to-be, remodeled from the old San Ysidro, the bare and grassless Mexican *plaza* changed to the square of a Kansas town, by tree and hard-won turf; blacksmith shop and school, with a little store and post office, clustered for company on one side: business would fill up the three blank sides—like Columbus or Cherryvale. For there is no new thing beneath the kindly sun. Not otherwise, far from the plains of windy Troy, did Priam's son build and copy, in the wild hills of Epirus:

> *The little Troy, the castle Pergamus,*
> *The river Xanthus, and the Scæan gate.*

Fringing the townlet, new gristmill and new factory stood where the mother ditch was bridged. Beyond the bridge the roads forked. From the right hand a steep cañon came plunging to the valley, winding dark between red-brown hills. This cañon was Redgate; here turned the climbing road to Upham; and Adam Forbes followed the Redgate road.

At the summit he turned to the left across a corner of MacCleod's Park; he crossed a whorl of low ridges at the head of Apache Cañon and came to Hidden Tanks—a little limestone basin, now brimming with rain-water, perhaps a dozen barrels in all. Adam had fenced this in with a combination of stone wall and cedar brush, to keep cattle out. He now climbed to a little low cliff near by. There he had cached his outfit in a little cupboard of a cave, the floor of it shoulder high to him where he stood. Here he unpacked. He added to the cache his little store of sugar, coffee, rice, bacon and flour, all packed in five or ten pound baking-powder cans against the ravages of mice, gray squirrels and trade rats. The little deep cave gave protection against larger pests and shelter from rain. He rolled up his bedding, lifted it into the mouth of the cave and shoved it back.

Two empty five-gallon kegs were left of his pack; he had not dared to leave them in the cache, to fall apart in the dry and sun-parched air. These kegs he filled at the tanks and slung on the pack saddle; with them he made his way to the hill of his hopes. It was close by; he had hidden there his pick, shovel and the broad shallow basin used for panning gold. He hobbled the horses; by ten o'clock, or a little later, he was deep in the interrupted task of a month before.

Freakish chance had timed that interruption to halt him on the very brink of success.

Before he had taken out a dozen pans he was in rich dirt. Noon found him shaken from the poise and mastery of years. Abandoning the patient and systematic follow-up system, he pushed on up the hill, sampling at random, and finding each sample richer. The scant supply of water was nearly gone, the gold frenzy clutched at his heart. By sighting, he roughly developed the lines showing the probable limit of pay dirt, as marked by the monuments of his earlier labor; he noted the intersection of those lines, and there began a feverish panning with his remnant of water. He found gold in flakes, in scales, in millet-seed grains—in grains like rice at last! He had tracked down a pocket to make history with, to count time from. And the last of his water was used.

Adam sat down, trembling to think his find had been unprotected by the shadow of a claim for the last month; reflected then that it had lain unclaimed for some thousands of years, and with the reflection pulled himself together and managed a grin at his own folly.

He went back to his saddle. Tucked in

the saddle pockets was a goodly lunch, but
he did not touch that. He untied his coat
and took out two printed location notices,
several crumply sheets of blank paper and a
pencil. He filled in the blanks as the location notice of the Goblin Gold Mine—original
notice and copy. On the blank paper he
wrote out four more notices, two originals and
two copies, for the Nine Bucks Placer Claim
and the Please Hush. For the Goblin Gold
he wrote himself as locator, Charles See and
Howard Lull as witnesses; he reserved this for
the highest and richest claim. For the next
below, Charles See was locator, Forbes and
Lull were witnesses; and the third was as-
signed to Howard Lull, with See and Forbes
to bear witness.

Adam paced off the three claims adjoining
each other and built a stone monument at each
corner, with a larger monument for the location-papers at the center of each claim; the
central monument of the Goblin Gold about
where he had made the last panning. And
then, even as he started to slip the first location
notice in its monument, he lifted up his eyes

and saw, across the tangled ridges, three men riding up from the deeps of Apache Cañon.

The cool judgment that had brought him safe through a thousand dangers was warped now by the fever and frenzy of gold lust; his canny instinct against disaster failed him in his need. There must be no shadow of irregularity on these claims, his hot brain reasoned; his find was too rich for chance-taking in the matter of mythical witnesses; yonder, by happy and unlooked for chance, were witnesses indeed; he must have their names to his location notices, and then he would get the copies to Hillsboro for recording at the earliest; he would mail them in Garfield post office that very afternoon.

He reversed his pencil and erased the names of his fictitious witnesses; he saddled his horse and rode to intercept the three horsemen, half a mile away now, trailing slowly across the park toward MacCleod's Tanks. He waved them to stop. As he drew near he knew two of the men—Jody Weir, of Hillsboro, and Big Ed Caney, a deputy sheriff from Dona Ana County; two men he trusted not at all. Time was he would have deemed this conjunction sinister; to-day, madness was upon him. The third was a stranger. Each man had a blanket and a bulging slicker tied behind his saddle. Evidently they carried rations for several days' camping.

"Hello, Adam!"

"You're another—three of 'em. Got any water in those canteens? If I was to do a piece of wishin', right now, I'd mention water first off. This is sure one old scorcher of a day! She's a weather breeder. Rain before morning, sure as snakes. I see thunderheads peeping up over the Black Range, right now."

Caney handed over a canteen. "Drink hearty! You shore look like you'd been working, Adam."

Adam drank deep before replying.

"Working is right. Prospecting. Tired of farming—need a change. Say, I want you fellows to witness some location notices for me. Ride over on the next ridge and I can point out where the claims lay so you can swear to 'em—or ride over with me if you got time. I was just doing a little forgery when

I saw your dust, for I wasn't expectin' to see a man up this way—not ever. I do reckon this is the lonesomest place in the world."

"Adam, meet my friend," said Jody. "Mr. Forbes, Mr. Hales. Now, Adam, no need for us to go over to your layout, is there? We can see your silly monuments. That's enough. No particular odds anyway, is it? I reckon half the notices on record have ghost signatures to 'em. Just as good as any. Nobody'll ever know the difference."

"Sure, that's all right—but seein' you happened along so slick, I thought I'd get your John Hancocks. Sign on the dotted line, please—where I rubbed out my forgeries."

"Any good, your mines?" asked Jody as they signed.

"Might be—will be, likely enough. Just struck pay dirt to-day. Lots of room if you want to try a whirl—all round my claims, any direction except down."

"Not to-day, I guess. Say, Forbes—you ain't seen any strangers this way, have you? Mexicans, mebbe?"

"Not any. But I just come up from the

river. Hills might be full of people, for all
I know. Water all round, after these rains."

"Look, now," said Jody. "We're doin' a
little man hunt—and if you're hangin' round
here prospectin', you may be able to give us a
straight tip. Keep your eye peeled. There'll
be a piece of money in it for you if you can
help us out."

"Give it a name. But see here, Caney—
this isn't Dona Ana County, you know.
You're over the line."

"I'm not doing this official," said Caney.
"Neither is Hales, here, though he is a deputy
in Socorro County. We're private cits in this
man's county—playin' a hunch. Here's the
lay: There's been a heap of stealing saddles
for a business lately—saddles and other truck,
but saddles, wholesale, most particular. Got
so it wasn't safe for a man to leave a saddle
on a horse at night, down round Las Cruces."

"They got Bill McCall's saddle in Mesilla
three months ago," broke in Jody, laughing.
"So Bill, he went and broke a bronc backward.
Yes, sir! Broke him to be saddled and
mounted from the wrong side. Only left-

handed horse in the world, I reckon. Then
Bill slips off down to Mesilla, ties his horse
in front of Isham Holt's house about dark,
and filters inside to jolly Miss Valeria.
Pretty soon Bill heard a tur'ble row outside,
and when he went out he found a Mex boy
rollin' round in the street and a-holdin' both
hands to his belly. Claimed he had the
cramps, he did—but that's why we're rather
looking for Mexicans."

"We figured they were a regular gang,
scattered up and down, hurrying the stuff
along by relays, and likely taking it down in
old Mexico to dispose of," said Caney.
"Then we hear that saddles are being missed
up in Socorro County too. So Hales and me
gets our wise heads together. Here is our
hugeous hunch: This is lonesome country
here, the big roads dodge the river from San
Marcial to Rincon, 'count of it being so rough,
so thieves wouldn't go by the Jornada nor yet
take the big west-side roads through Palomas
or Hillsboro. No, sir. They just about follow the other side of the river, where nobody
lives, as far down as Engle Ferry. There or

thereabouts they cross over, climb up Mescal
Cañon and ooze out through the rough country
east of Caballo Mountain. Then they either
come through by MacCleod's and cross the
river here again, or they keep on down below
Rincon to Barela Bosque. Maybe they save
up till they get a wagonload of saddles, cover
them up with a tarp or maybe some farm
truck, and drive whistlin' down the big road to
El Paso."

"Anyhow," said Hales, "the Cattle Association has offered an even thousand for information leading to conviction, and we're going to watch the passes and water holes—here
and at Hadley Spring and Palomas Gap. If
you help get the thousand, you help spend it.
That's right, ain't it, boys?"

The others nodded.

"Go with you, you mean?"

"No. You stay here—so long as you're
here anyway—while we ride up the line.
That way, one of us can go on and watch
Mescal. We was one man shy before," said
Caney. "Does it go?"

"It goes."

"Take your silly location papers then, and we'll ride.   We're going across to have a look for tracks in Deadman first."   He jerked his chin toward a notch in the hills, halfway between the head of Apache Cañon and the head of Redgate.   "Then we'll go up by Mac-Cleod's Tank and on through to the Jornada and up the east side of Timber Mountain."

"Me, I reckon I'll post my notice and then go mail the copies to the recorder's office," said Adam.   "Thank'ee, gentlemen. *Adios!*"

Jody Weir pulled up his horse behind the first hill.

"Fellers, that man has made a strike! Didya see his face—all sweat and dust? Adam Forbes is not the man to rustle like that in this broiling sun unless he was worked up about something.   He didn't act natural, nohow.   He drawls his talk along, as a usual thing—but to-day he spoke up real crisp and peart.   I tell you now, Forbes has found the stuff!"

"I noticed he didn't seem noways keen for

us to go help post his papers," said Caney.

"Humph! I began noticin' before that," said Toad Hales. "Us signing as witnesses— that got my eye.   Usually it makes no never minds about a witness to a mining claim. They sign up John Smith, Robinson Crusoe or Jesse James, and let it go at that.   Mighty strict and law-abiding all of a sudden, he was! And going to record his papers the day of dis- covery—when he has ninety days for it?   It's got all the earmarks of a regular old he-strike! I move we take rounders on him and go look- see."

"Cowboy—you done said something."

They slipped back furtively, making a de- tour, riding swiftly under cover of shielding hills; they peeped over a hill crest beyond Adam's claims just in time to see him riding slowly away in the direction of Redgate.

"Gone to mail his notices to Hillsboro!" snarled Jody.   "Some hurry!   Come on, you —let's look into this."

They found pick and pan, stacked with the empty water kegs by the location monument of the Goblin Gold; they scraped up a small

pan of dirt from one of the shallow holes of
Adam's making; they poured in water from
their canteens; Caney did the washing. He
poured off the lighter dirt, he picked out the
pebbles, he shook the residue with a gentle
oscillating movement; he poured the muddy
water cautiously, he shook the pan again.

"Sufferin' tomcats!" yelled Hales. "Gold
as big as wheat!"

Caney's face went whitey-green; he completed the washing with a last dexterous flirt
and set down the pan with trembling hands.

"Look at that!"

Jody's eyes were popping from his head.
"A pocket! Even if it plays out in a day—
a day's work would make us rich for life!"

"Us—hell!" said Caney. "We get the
crumbs and leavings. Adam Forbes knows
what he's about. He's got the cream. Outside of his claims the whole damn mountain
won't be worth hell room!"

Jody turned his eyes slowly toward Redgate. "If we'd only known we might have
horned in. Three of us—why, sooner than

lose it all and get himself killed to boot, we might have split this fifty-fifty."

"We'll split this thirty-thirty!" Caney sprang to his feet. "Have you got the guts for it? Jody, this is your country—can we head him off?"

"If he goes round by the head of Redgate Cañon—and if we don't stay here talking— we can cut across through Deadman. There's a pass where Deadman and Redgate bend close together. It won't be a long shot—two hundred yards."

"Three shots! Come on!" Hales swung on his horse. "We've all got our rifles. Three shots! Come on!" He jabbed the spurs home.

It was not until they had passed the park that the others overtook Hales.

"Here, you, Hales—don't kill your horse!" said Jody Weir. "If he beats us to the pass we're not done yet. He'll come back to-night. He said so."

"You cussed fool! If he once gets those location notices in the mail we might as well let him go. We couldn't take the chances and get by with it."

"That's just it," said Jody. "Hi! Caney! Ride up alongside. Slow up, Hales! Listen, both of you. Even if he gets those papers in the mail, the recorder need never see them. All I have to do is to say the word. I'm on the inside—sure and safe."

"Sure?"

"Sure and safe. If he beats us to the gap and comes back—well, you stop Adam's mouth and I'll be responsible for the papers. They'll never be recorded in this world!"

"Where's your stand-in? At Garfield?"

"Never you mind my stand-in. That's my lookout. A letter posted at Garfield to-night goes to Rincon by buckboard to-morrow; it lays over in Rincon to-morrow night, goes out on the High Line to Nutt on the nine-fifteen day after to-morrow, takes the branch line to Lake Valley, and goes from Lake to Hillsboro by stage. It don't get to Hillsboro till two in the afternoon, day after to-morrow. It takes as long from Garfield to Hillsboro as from Chicago. After—after—if we turn the trick—we can come back and post location notices for ourselves.   Then we can beat it on a bee line for Hillsboro and record 'em."

"Aha! So it's at Hillsboro post office you're the solid Muldoon, is it?"

Weir's gun flashed to a level with Caney's breast. "That will be all from you, Caney! Your next supposing along those lines will be your last. Get me? Now or ever! Keep your mouth closed, and Adam Forbes' mouth. That's your job."

"Put up your gun, kid.   I can't afford to be killed. I'm going to be a howlin' million-aire. I'll say no more, but I'm not sorry I spoke. You bein' so very earnest that way, I'm satisfied you can deliver the goods.   That is what I want to know—for I tell you now, I don't expect to head Forbes off here.   He had too much start of us—unless he dilly-dallies along the road or is delayed."

"If he comes back, won't he bring a gang with him? If he does we're done," said Hales.   "That's why I'm willing to kill my horse to beat him to it.   You two seem more interested in chewing the rag."

"O, that's all right! Jody and me, we've come to a good understanding," said Caney smoothly. Jody Weir glanced carelessly at the back of Hales' head, his eyes wandered till they met Caney's eyes and held steadily there for a moment; his brows arched a trifle.

"Well, here we are," announced Jody. "We'd better make the climb afoot. The horses are about done and they'd make too much noise anyway—floundering about. It's all slick rock."

They took their rifles from the saddles, they clambered up the steep pass, they peered over cautiously.

"Hell! There's two of them!" said Caney. "Get 'em both! Big stakes! This is the chance of a lifetime!"

Below them on a little shelf of promontory stood a saddled horse, a blue horse. A yearling was hog-tied there, and a branding fire burned beside. As they looked, a young man knelt over the yearling and earmarked it. Close by, Adam Forbes slouched in the saddle, leaning with both hands on the horn. He

gave a letter to the young man, who stuck it
into his shirt and then went back to the yearling. He loosed the hogging-string. The
yearling scrambled to his feet, bawling de-
fiance, intent on battle; the young man
grabbed the yearling's tail and jerked him
round till his head faced down the cañon.
Adam Forbes made a pass with his horse and
slapped with his hat; the yearling fled.

"Wait! Wait!" whispered Jody. "I know
that man! That's Johnny Dines. Wait!
Adam wants to get back and feel that gold in
his fingers. Ten to one Dines is going across
the river; I can guess his business; he's hunting for the John Cross. Adam gave him the
location-papers to mail. If Adam goes back
—there's your scapegoat—Dines! He'll be
the man that killed Forbes!"

"Friend of yours, Jody?"

"Damn him! If they both start down the
cañon, you fellows get Forbes. I'll get Dines
myself. That's the kind of friend he is. Get
your guns ready—they'll be going in a minute,
one way or the other."

"Curiously enough, I know Johnny Dines myself," muttered Hales. "Very intelligent man, Dines. Very! I would take a singular satisfaction in seeing young Dines hung. To that laudable end I sure hope your Mr. Forbes will not go down the cañon."

"Well, he won't! Didn't you see him give Dines the papers?" said Caney. "Lay still! This is going to match up like clockwork."

The men below waved their hands to each other in friendly fashion; Forbes jogged lazily up the cañon; Dines stamped out the branding fire and rode whistling on the riverward road.

"Weir, you're dead sure you can pull the trick about the papers? All right, then—you and Hales go over there and write out joint location papers in the names of the three of us. Got a pencil? Yes? Burn the old notices, and burn 'em quick. Burn his kegs and turn his hobbled horse loose. We will bring his tools as we come back, and hide 'em in the rocks. Any old scrap of paper will do us. Here's some old letters. Use the backs of them. After we get to Hillsboro we'll make copies to file."

These directions came jerkily and piece-meal as the conspirators scrambled down the hillside.

"Where'll we join you?"

Caney paused with his foot in the stirrup to give Jody Weir a black look.

"I'll join you, young fellow, and I'll join you at our mine. Do you know, I don't alto-gether trust you? I want to see those two sets of location papers with my two eyes before we start. So you'll have lots of time. Don't you make no mistakes. And when we go, we go together. Then if we happen to find Adam Forbes by the fire where he caught young Dines stealin' a maverick of his—"

"How'll you manage that? Forbes is half-way to the head of the cañon by now."

"That's your way to the left, gentlemen. Take your time, now. I'm in no hurry and you needn't be, and our horses are all tired from their run. And you want to be most mighty sure you keep on going. For the next half hour nobody's going to know what I'm doing but me and God—and we won't tell."

Caney turned off to the right. Fifteen minutes later he met Adam Forbes in a tangle of red hills by the head of Redgate.

"Hi, Adam! We got 'em!" he hailed jubilantly. "Caught 'em with the goods. Two men and five saddles. Both Mexicans."

"They must have given you one hell of a chase, judging from your horse."

"They did. We spied 'em jest over the divide at the head of Deadman. There wasn't any chance to head 'em off. We woulda tagged along out of sight, but they saw us first. They dropped their lead horses and pulled out —but we got close enough to begin foggin' lead at 'em in a straight piece of cañon, and they laid 'em down."

"Know 'em?"

"Neither one. Old Mexico men, I judge by the talk of 'em. Hales and Jody took 'em on down Deadman—them and the lead horses —while I come back for you."

"Me? Whadya want o' me?"

"Why, you want to go down to represent for yourself. You know that odd bit of land, grown up to brush, that you bought of Miguel Silva?"

"Took it on a bad debt.   What of it?"

"Why, there's an old tumbledown shack on it, and they've been using that as a store house, tha'sall.   By their tell they got eighteen assorted saddles hid there."

"Well, I'm damned!" said Adam, turning back.   "That's a blame fine howdy-do, ain't it?   How long have they been at this lay?"

"Four or five months.   More'n that south of here.   But they just lately been extendin' and branchin' out."

"Making new commercial connections, so to speak.   Any of the Garfield *gente* implicated?"

"One.   Albino Villa Neuva."

Adam nodded.   "Always thought he was a bad *hombre,* Albino."

"They're going to come clean, these two," said Caney cheerfully.   "We told 'em if they'd turn state's evidence they'd probable get off light.   Reckon we're going to round up the whole gang.   Say, I thought you'd hiked on to Garfield. I started back to your little old mine, cut into your sign, and was followin' you up."

"Yes, I did start down all right. But I met up with a lad down here a stretch and give him my papers and shackled on back. Damn your saddle thieves, anyway—I sure wanted to go back and paw round that claim of mine. My pack horse is back there hobbled, too."

"Aw, nemmine your pack horse. He'll make out till mornin'."

Ahead of them the wagon road was gouged into the side of an overhang of promontory, under a saddleback pass to northward. A dim trail curved away toward the pass. Adam's eye followed the trail. Caney's horse fell back a step.

"There's where I found my mail carrier," said Adam; "up on top of that little thumb. A Bar Cross waddy, he was—brandin' a calf."

Caney fired three times. The muzzle of his forty-five was almost between Adam's shoulders. Adam fell sidewise to the left, he clutched at his rifle, he pulled it with him as he fell. His foot hung in the stirrup, his horse dragged him for a few feet. Then his foot came free. He rolled over once, and tried to pull his rifle up. Then he lay still with his face in the dust.

VIII

"IT is a hard world," sighed Charlie See. "Life is first one thing and then it is a broom factory."

They made a gay cavalcade of laughter and shining life, those four young people. They had been to show Charlie over the gristmill and the broom factory, new jewels in Garfield's crown, and now they turned from deed to dream, rode merry for a glimpsing of tomorrow, where Hobby Lull planned a conquest more lasting than Cæsar's. Their way led now beyond the mother ditch to lands yet unredeemed, which in the years to come would lie under a high ditch yet to be. So they said and thought. But what in truth they rode forth for to see was east of the sun and west of the moon—not to be told here. Where youth rides with youth under a singing sky the chronicle should be broad-spaced between the lines; a double story, word and silence.

162

To what far-off divine event we move, there shall be no rapture keener than hoping time in unspoiled youth.

The embankments of the mother ditch were head-high to them as they rode. They paused on the high bridge between the desert and the sown. Behind lay the broad and level clearings, orchard, kempt steading and alfalfa; a step beyond was the raw wilderness, the yucca and the sand, dark mesquite in hummocks and mottes and clumps, a brown winding belt between the mother ditch and the first low bench land. The air came brisk and sweet; it rippled the fields to undulant shimmer of flashing purple and green and gold.

"Your *'cequia madre* is sure brimful this evenin'," remarked the guest.

"Always is—when we don't need it. In dry weather she gets pretty low enough," said Hobby. "Colorado people get the first whack at the water, and New Mexico takes what is left. Never high water here except at flood time. Fix that different some day. We got to fight flood and drought now, one down, another come on. Some day we'll save the flood water. Sure! No floods, no drought. Easy as lying! *Vamonos!*"

The road followed the curving ditch; their voices were tuned to lipping water and the drone of bees. Lull pointed out the lines where his high ditch was to run at the base of the bench land, with flume at gully and cañon steeps. As eye and mapping hand turned toward Redgate a man came down Redgate road to meet them; a man on a Maltese horse. He rode briskly, poised, sure-swaying as ever bird on bough. Charlie See warmed to the lithe youth of him.

"There, fellow citizens," he said, "there is what I'd call a good rider!"

As the good rider came abreast he swept off his hat. His eyes were merry; he nodded greeting and shook back a mop of blackest hair. The sun had looked upon him. He checked the blue horse in his stride—not to stop, but to slow him; he spoke to Lull in passing.

"Garfield post office?" He jerked a thumb toward the bridge; for indeed, seen across the ramparts of the ditch, there was small distinction between visible Garfield and the scattered farmsteads. "This way?"

"Yes."

"Just across the bridge," added Lyn. The story scorns to suppress the truth—she smiled her dimpliest.

"Thanks," said the stranger; and then, as he came abreast of Charlie See: "And the road to Hillsboro? Back this way—or straight on?"

"Straight through. Take the right hand at the post office—straight to the ford. You'll have to swim, I reckon."

"Yes," said the stranger indifferently. He was well beyond See and Edith Harkey now, and the blue horse came back into the road and into his reaching stride. "Thanks." The stranger looked back with the last word; at the same time Miss Dyer turned her head. They smiled.

"And they turned Lot's wife into a pillar of salt!" said Mr. Lull bitterly.

"He had such smiling eyes," urged Lyn.

"Ruin and destruction! See! Edith! Spread out—head her off!" Hobby grabbed Lyn's bridle rein and led his captive away at a triumphant trot.

They turned aside to inspect the doubtful passage where the future ditch must clamber and twist to cross Deadman; Hobby Lull explained, defended, expounded; he bristled with estimates, alternative levels and acre costs; here was the inevitable way, but yonder there was a choosing; at that long gray point, miles away, the ditch must leave the river to gain the needed grades. He sparkled with irresistible enthusiasm, he overbore opposition.

"Look here, folks!" said Hobby. "See those thunder-heads? It's clouding up fast. It's going to rain and there's not a man in town can stop it. I aimed to take you up and show you the place we picked to make the ditch head, but I judge we best go home. We can see the ditch head another day."

"Now was I convinced or only persuaded?" Charlie See made the grumbling demand of Edith as they set their faces homeward.

Yet he was secretly impressed; he paused by jungle and sandy swale or ribbed and gullied slope for admiration of orchards unplanted and friendly homesteads yet to be; he drew rein by a pear thicket and peered half enviously into its thorny impenetrable keeps.

"Who lives there, Edith? That's the best place we've seen. Big fine house and all, but it looks comfortable and homey, just the same —mighty pleasant and friendly. And them old-fashioned flower beds are right quaint."

"Hollyhocks," she breathed; "and marigolds, and four o'clocks. An old-fashioned woman lives here."

Charlie's voice grew wistful. "I might have had a place like this just as well as not— if I'd only had sense enough to hear and hark. Hobby Lull brought me out here and put me wise, years ago, but I wouldn't listen. There was a bunch of us. Hobby and—and—now who else was it? It was a merry crowd, I can remember that. Hobby did all the talking— but who were the others? And have they forgotten too? It was a long time ago, before the big ditch. Oh, dear! I do wish I could remember who was with me!"

His voice trailed off to silence and a sigh
that was only half assumed.

"You make it seem very real," she said, unconscious of her answering deeper sigh.

"Real. It is real! Look there—and there—
and there!"

"That is all Hobby's work," said Edith as
her eyes followed his pointing finger, and saw
there what he saw—the city of his vision, the
courts and palaces of love. "He has the
builder's mind."

"Yes. It is a great gift." It was said un-
grudgingly. "I wish I had it. That way lies
happiness. Me—I am a spectator."

She shook her reins to go, with a last look
at his phantom farmlands. "'An' I 'a stubb'd
Thurnaby waäste.' That's what they'll put on
Hobby's tombstone."

She lifted up her eyes from the waste places
and the seeming, and let them rest on the
glowing mesas beyond the river and the long
dim ridges of misty mountain beyond and over
all; and saw them in the light that never was
on sea or land. The heart of the good warm

boisterous earth called to kindred clay, "and turned her sweet blood into wine."

Shy happiness tinged her pale cheek with color, a tint of wild rose and sea-shell delicacy, faint and all unnoted; he was half inattentive to her as she rode beside him, glowing in her splendid spring, a noble temple of life, a sanctuary ready for clean sacrifice.

"Yes. Hobby, he's all right. Him and his likes, they put up the brains and take the risks and do the work. But after it's all done some of these austere men we read about, they'll ooze in and gather the crops."

"He doesn't miss much worth having. What may be weighed and counted and stolen and piled in heaps—oh, yes, Hobby Lull may miss that. Not real things, like laughter and joy and—and love, Charlie."

Charlie See turned his head toward Redgate. She read his thought; in her face the glow of life faded behind the white skin. But he did not see it; nor the thread of pain in her eyes. In his thought she was linked with Adam Forbes, and at her word he smiled to think of his friend, and looked up to Redgate where, even then, "Nicanor lay dead in his harness."

Pete Harkey's buckboard stood by the platform in front of the little store, and the young people waited there for him and his marketing.

"Mail day?" asked Charlie.

"Nope. To-morrow is the big day."

"We used to get it three times a week," said Lyn. "Now it's only twice."

"When I was a boy," said See thoughtfully, "I always wanted to rob a stage, just once. Somehow or other I never got round to it." His brow clouded.

"Why, Mr. See!"

"Charlie," said Mr. See. "Well, you needn't be shocked. Society is very unevenly divided between the criminal and the non-criminal classes."

"That," said Edith, "might be called a spiral remark. Would it be impertinent to ask you to specify?"

"Not at all. Superfluous. See for your-

self. Old Sobersides, here—you might give
him the benefit of the doubt—he's so durned
practical. But Adam and me, Uncle Dan
and your Dad—there's no doubt about us,
I'm afraid. It's right quaint to see how proud
those old roosters are of the lurid past. When
one of 'em gets on the peck, all you got to do
is to start relatin' how wild they used to be, and
they'll be eatin' out of your hand in no time.
They ought to be ashamed of themselves—silly
old donkeys!"

"How about the women?" asked Lyn.

"I've never been able to make a guess. But
there's so few of you out here at the world's
end, that you don't count for much, either
way."

"Lyn realizes that," said Hobby. "Here at
the ragged edge of things she knows that the
men outnumber the women five to one. So
she tries to make up for it. She is a friendly
soul."

Miss Lyn Dyer ignored this little speech
and harked back to the last observation of
Charlie See. "So you did manage to notice
that, did you? I'm surprised. They've

amused me for years—Uncle Dan and Uncle Pete; how mean they were, the wild old days and the chimes at midnight! But a girl—oh, dear me, how very different! No hoydens need apply! A notably unwild boy is reproached as a sissy and regarded with suspicion, but a girl must not even play at being wild. 'Prunes, prisms and potatoes!' Podsnap! Pecksniff! Turveydrop and Company! Doesn't anyone ever realize that it might be a tame business never to be wild at all?"

" 'Tis better to be wild and weep—"

"Now, Hobby Lull, you hush up! The answer is, No. Catechism. A man expects from his womankind a scrupulous decorum which he is far too broad-minded to require from himself or his mates—charitable soul! Laughter and applause. Cries of 'That's true!'—Anything more grossly unfair—"

Rub-a-dub! Rub-a-dub! Rub-a-dub!

Three men thundered over the *'cequia* bridge. At the first drum of furious hoofs See wheeled his horse sharply.

"What's that? Trouble!" The three

horsemen swooped from the bridge, pounding
on the beaten road. "Trouble, sure!"

"You two girls light out of this! Ride!"
said Lull. He spurred to the open door of
the store. "Pete!" he called, and turned back.

"Adam?" said Charlie. "Something wrong
up Redgate way. Adam's there, and no one
else that we know of."

"I'm afraid so. Horse fell on him maybe
—dynamite or something. Here they come.
Big Ed and Jody Weir. I don't know the
third man."

The horsemen were upon them. "Murder!" cried Caney. "Adam Forbes has been
murdered! Up in Redgate. The murderer
came this way. We trailed him to the bridge.
His horse had lost a shoe."

"Adam Forbes!"

"Who is to tell Edith?" said Charlie See,
under his breath.

"Someone's going to hang for this. When
we found him—I never had such a shock in
my life!" said Jody Weir. "Shot from behind—three times. The powder burned his
shirt. Adam never had a chance. Cold-

blooded murder. Adam was holding fast to his rifle, wrong side up, just as he pulled it from the scabbard. That man came through here."

"Or stopped here," amended Caney. "Might have been a Garfield man, of course. I've heard that Forbes was tol'able arbitrary."

"We met a stranger coming down from Redgate, something like an hour and a half ago," said Hobby. "But if he had just killed a man, I'll eat my hat. That man was feeling fine. Only a boy, too. Someone else did it, I guess."

"And he'd been riding slow. No sweat on his horse," added Charlie.

"Couldn't have been anyone else. There wasn't any other tracks, except the tracks of Adam's horse. They turned off south as soon as he got out of the mouth of the cañon."

"How'd you know it was Adam's horse?" This was Pete Harkey, at the open door.

"Saw where the bridle reins dragged. Say! Any you fellows comin' with us? That man killed Forbes, I tell you—and we're goin' after him. Only about two hours till dark—two and a half at most—and a rain coming up. This is no time for talking. We can talk on the road."

"Anybody stay with Adam?" asked Pete.

"No. There was just the three of us. We came full chisel after the murderer, hard as we could ride. Come on—get some of your men together—let's ride," said Caney impatiently. "Get a wiggle on, can't you? Let's find out which way he went and what he looked like. He came here. No chance for mistake. The body was still warm."

"I saw him! I saw him!" cackled the storekeeper. "Little man, smaller than Charlie— and young. About twenty. Came in after you all left," he said, addressing Lull. "Mailed a letter. Ridin' a blue horse, he was —a *grullo*. That the man you met?"

"Yes. But riding a blue horse doesn't prove that a man has done murder. Nor yet mailing a letter. Or being young. We knew that man went through Garfield. That's nothing new. He told us he was going on to Hillsboro."

"That was a blind, I reckon. He can turn

always back, soon as he gets out of sight," said Hales.

"He went that way," piped the storekeeper. "Mailed a letter here, bought a shoe and tacked it on his horse. I fished round to find out who he was, but he put me off. Finally I asked him, p'int-blank. 'You didn't say what your name was,' says I. 'No,' says he, 'I didn't.' And off he went, laughing, impydent as hell!"

"Did you notice the brand on his horse?" asked Charlie. "He passed on our right-hand side, so we didn't see it."

"No, I didn't. He took the Greenhorn road, and he was ridin' middlin' slow."

"If you had used your mouth less and your eyes more, you might have something to tell us," sneered Hales.

"Little man on a *grullo* horse—that's enough for us—we're goin'!" snapped Caney. "Say, you fellers make me plumb sick! The murderer's getting away, and all you do is blat. We're goin', and we're goin' now!"

"Something tells me you won't," said Pete Harkey.

He had mysteriously acquired a shotgun from his buckboard, and he cocked both hammers with the word. "Not till we talk a little. According to your tell, the killing was done in Sierra County. That's my county, and we figure we are plenty competent to skin our own skunks. Also, we want one good long look before we leap. You three are the only men who can tell us anything, and we want to know what you know, so we'll not lose time or make mistakes. We can't afford to shoot so as to hit if it's a deer and miss if it's a mule. You fellers are excited. What you need is a head. I'll be head.

"You just calm down a little. I'll be getting a posse together to go back and look into this. You can be fixing to give us some idea what's happened. After that, these two boys can go with you. They've seen this stranger and they'll know him on a fresh horse. All you three know about his looks is a blue horse. I'm going up where Adam was killed. Where was it? Don't be nervous about this gun. I never shot a man accidentally in my life. Where was Adam killed?"

"In Redgate. Near the upper end. We was looking—"

"That's enough. You wait till I send for some friends of mine." Pete raised his voice. "Girls! Ride over here! Now you folks keep still till the girls get away. Toad Hales, is it? I've seen you before, Mr. Hales. . . . Edith, you go to the mill and tell Jerome I want him. Lyn, you go to Chuck Barefoot's and tell him to get Jim-Ike-Jones and come here and be quick about it. Then you girls go home."

"What is it, Uncle Pete? Adam?" said Lyn, with a quivering lip.

"Yes, dear. Go on, now."

"Dead?"

"Murdered!"

"Adam!"

Both girls cried the name in an agony of horror and pity. Edith bent to her horse's mane; and Lyn rode straight to Hobby Lull.

"Oh, Hobby! Be careful—come back to me!" She raised her lips to his. He took her in his arms and kissed her; she clung to him, shaken with sobbing. "Oh, poor Adam!" She cried. "Poor Adam!"

Charlie See turned away. For one heart beat of flinching his haunted soul looked from his eyes; then with a gray courage, he set his lips to silence. If his face was bleak—why not, for Adam, his friend?

And Edith Harkey, on her sad errand, envied the happy dead. She, alone of them all, had seen that stricken face.

"Lyn, you go on," said Pete. "Get Barefoot. Then go home and find out where your Uncle Dan is, and send him along just as fast as ever God'll let him come."

He turned back to the men.

"Now, then, you fellows! Begin at the beginning. Hales, you didn't know Adam, so you won't be so bad broke up as the others. Suppose you tell us what you know. Wait a minute. Sam, you be saddling up a horse for me. Now, Mr. Hales?"

"We were looking out for that gang of saddle thieves. Went up 'Pache Cañon. Along in the park we saw tracks where two shod horses turned down into Redgate, and we followed them up. One of 'em had been chasing a bunch of cattle—or so we thought, though we didn't notice that part very close, having no particular reason for it then. We'd looked through two-three bunches of cattle ourselves earlier, for Jody's stuff."

"Yes, and you had breakfast, likely—but what do I care? You get on with your story."

"Say, old man," said Hales in some exasperation, "if you don't want this man caught, I'm satisfied. It's nothing to me. I didn't know Forbes. If you want this friend of yours to get away, I'm willing to get down and stay all night. You're pretty overbearing with your little old shotgun."

He made as if to dismount.

"Oh, I wouldn't do that," said Pete mildly. "Look at your friends, first. They're just as overborne as you are, likely—but you notice they are not making any complaints. They know me, you see. They know how Adam Forbes stood in Garfield, and what kind of folks live in Garfield; and they know that whoever killed Adam is in trouble up to his neck. You mustn't mind our little ways.

Courtesy Ruth Koerner Oliver

Shotgun and the Law

However, as the witness is peeved, we'll try another.   Jody, speak up and tell us."

"You act like we was under suspicion," sneered Hales.

"Sure, you're under suspicion! What do you expect? Everybody's under suspicion till we find the right man.   I'm going to send word up and down to hold all strangers. That part is all right.   Hello, Jerome! You missed most of the evidence! I'll tell you about it as we go up."

"Now why the little gun?" said Jerome Martin, tranquilly.

"Been holding an election. Now, Jody— your little piece."

"There's not much to tell. We found Adam's body a little ways down the cañon, maybe a quarter or a little more; and just this side of it we found where a yearling had been branded, or a big calf; ashes still warm. Looks just like this fellow had been stealing one of Adam's calves, and Adam caught him at it."

"But you said Adam was shot in the back at close range," objected Charlie.   "Adam

Forbes wouldn't turn his back to any man, under those circumstances. That won't work."

"Yes, we thought of that," said Caney. "More likely he saw Adam coming and killed him before he got to the calf—pretending to be friendly. Anyhow, Adam's horse went off down the cañon, and the other man went down the cañon, and we came after him. Oh, yes! His horse lost a shoe, as we told you before—the murderer's. Must have lost it chasing that calf. Tracks didn't show it in the soft ground in the park, anyhow—though we didn't look very close till we found Adam. But after he left Adam's body his tracks showed one shoe gone. That's all. Adam's horse bore off to the left. He had a larger foot than the other, and we could see where the bridle dragged."

"I'll send someone to find him. You didn't hear any shots?"

"Oh, no—we just thought maybe we'd meet up with some puncher ridin' the range, and ask him had he seen any strangers. This gang of saddle thieves—"

"Yes, I know about them. Thankee, gentlemen. You can ride now. If you catch your man beyond the river you might as well take him on to Hillsboro. Be mighty sure to remember not to forget to be particular to take this young man alive. We want to hang the man that killed Adam Forbes. That's all."

"Here, I want some cartridges," said Hobby. He leaped off and jingled into the store. "Hi, Sam! Get me a box of forty-fives," he called. Then to Harkey, in a guarded voice: "Pete, this looks fishy as hell! Those ashes were warm, they said. Look what time it is now—half past four. The way they were riding, this bunch made it from Redgate in half an hour. We met this stranger near two hours ago. That don't hold together. If the stranger man built that fire, the ashes would have been cold when Caney's bunch found them. And they say there are no other tracks. Wrong—all wrong!"

"And all the rest of it. Son, I didn't miss a bet. Neither did Charlie See. He looked hard at me. Save your breath. Say nothing and see everything. You do your part and I'll do mine. I'll know more before dark if it don't rain and rub out the tracks. Our Father which is in Garfield hates a lie, and he's fixed up this here solar system so there is no safe place in it for a lie. Sh-h! Here comes Caney!" He raised his voice. "What the devil do you need of more men? Five to one —what more do you want?"

"Well, but we may lose track of him and want to spread out to look and ask, while some of us go on—"

"Where can I find drinking water?" asked Caney.

"Back there," said Pete, pointing. Then, to Hobby: "Well, pick up someone in Arrey, then, or on the way. I want the men round here to go with me and look round before it gets dark. Say, Sam—you send someone up with a wagon to bring Adam back, will you? I'm off—me and Jerome. Tell Jones and Barefoot to come right on. Take care of my team for me."

He went out on the platform. Lull and Caney followed.

"Well, so long, you fellows," said Pete.
"Send word back if you find your man. Because there's going to be a lot of irritated
strangers when we start to picking them up."

"We had some plunder—grub and a blanket
apiece tied behind our saddles, and we
dumped it, to ride light, where we found
Adam—just kept our slickers," said Caney.
"Have 'em bring 'em in, will you, Harkey?"

"Sure," said Pete.

IX

"This to the crowd—speak bitter, proud and high,
But simply to your friend—she loves you not!"
                              —*Le Bret—who scolds.*

THE five pursuers rode swiftly, with inquiry at several farms about the man on the blue horse. Some had seen him; some had not. He had been riding slowly and he had kept the main road to Greenhorn. They took the Greenhorn Island ford and found good swimming. The quarry had passed through Donahue's an hour and a half before, taking the road to Arrey. They pushed on furiously. See and Lull fell behind a little.

"Say, this is a rotten deal!" said Charlie. "That man ain't running away. Not on your life. He no more killed Adam Forbes than I did. You know how long ago we met him. If he was the man that built that branding fire, how does it happen the ashes were still hot when these fellows found it? By their tell and our timing that was near three hours later.

We met him about three; if he made that fire it couldn't have been later than two o'clock, by the looks of his horse. And he's keeping the same steady gait, and going straight for Hillsboro, just as he told us. We're gaining on him right along. He's not trying to get away. Either he's innocent or he's got the devil's own nerve."

"Innocent. Pete thinks so, too. This crowd tells a fishy story. Did you notice how prompt Caney was to explain why they was there, and why they went down Redgate, and why the stranger shot Adam, and how Adam gave him a chance to shoot him in the back? Always Caney! Say, Hob, that man was too willing by half!"

"And that excitement. I wasn't surprised at Jody, and I don't know this man Hales— but wouldn't you think Ed Caney had seen enough men killed not to fight his head like that? He didn't have much use for Adam, either. Adam backed him down once. It was kept quiet, but Anastacio told me, on the dead. It tickled Anastacio. No, sir—those three fellows acted like they might be wishin' to start a stampede.   I'm not satisfied a little bit."

"A grudge?   But if one of these ducks is in, they're all in.   This is something else. Or of course it may have been some other person altogether, and these people may have merely lost their heads.   Do you reckon that placer hunt of Adam's might have had anything to do with it?   Poor old Adam!   We'll find time to grieve for him after we get the man that rubbed him out."

"I can't hardly realize it.   It won't come home to us till we've seen him, I expect.   I keep saying it over to myself—'Adam's dead' —but I don't believe it.   And only last night Edith sang that nightingale song after him— poor kid!   Say—look at that, will you? You'd think Caney didn't dare trust us to talk together."

Caney dropped back to them.

"Can't you two get any action out of them horses of yourn?" he snarled.   "It'll soon be dark on us.   Your horses are enough sight fresher than ours."

Charlie See jumped his horse up and reined

him to his haunches beside Caney, eye to eye;
he cocked his hat athwart.

"Now, Mr. Ed Caney," he said sweetly,
"any time you're not just satisfied with the way
I behave you know what you can do. This
place is here and this time is now. Fly to
it!"

"Why, what's eating you, Charlie? This
spitfire - wildcat - wolf - and - my - night - to - howl
thing is a new lay, isn't it?   I always gave you
credit for some sense."

"Your mistake," said Charlie. "You ride
on. I don't like deputy sheriffs much; especially deputies from Dona Ana; and most
extra special and particular, tall deputies from
Dona Ana with their faces pitted with small-
pox, going by the name of Ed Caney, and
butting into my private conversation. Me
and old Stargazer will be in at the finish, and
we don't need anybody to tell us how fast to
go or nothing like that at all. So what are
you going to do about it?"

"I'm going to ride on—that's what!" said
Caney. "You can come along or you can go
to hell—I don't care."

"It's a cruel world," said Charlie. "I've heard people call you a fool, but I know better, now. Don't you worry about us not keeping up."

Caney drove home the spurs and drew ahead.

They galloped into Arrey.

Yes, they had seen a man on a blue horse. "Filled his canteen here. Peart pair! . . . Which way? Oh, right up the big road to Hillsb'ro—him singin' and the horse dancin'. . . . Oh, maybe half an hour ago. He stayed here quite some time—admirin' the mountains, I judge, and fillin' his canteen—him and Josie. Better stay to supper, you-all; looks mighty like rain over yonder."

They turned squarely from the river valley and pushed up the staircase road. The track was clear and plain, three old shoes and a new one. They climbed the first bench-land step, and saw the long gray road blank before them in the last flame-red of sun. Swift dusk dropped like a curtain as they climbed the next step and saw a slow black speck far ahead in the dim loneliness.

"Got him!" said Jody. "Here, one can trail along behind, while two of us take the right and two go on the left, keeping cover in little draws and behind ridges. We'll have him surrounded before he knows we're after him. Way he's riding, we can head him off long before he gets to the Percha."

"Fine!" said Hobby Lull. "Fine! He rides into an ambush at dark. Guilty—he fights of course. Innocent—of course he fights! Any man with a bone in his spinal column would fight. First-rate scheme, except that Charlie See and me won't have it. Innocent, it isn't hospitable; guilty, we won't have him shot. The man that killed Adam Forbes has got to hang."

Leaping, Charlie See's horse whirled on a pivot and faced the others.

"Speed up, Hobby, and tell that man we're holding all strangers, him most of all. I'll hold this bunch. Beat it!"

His voice was low and drawling; he barred the way with quiet steady eyes. The storm-drenched wind blew out his saddle strings, the fringed edges of his gauntlets, the kerchief at his neck, the long tapideros at his feet; it beat back his hat's broad brim, Stargazer's mane snapped loose and level; horse and man framed against coming night and coming storm in poised wild energy, centered, strong and tense.

"You darned little meddlesome whiffet!" snarled Jody Weir savagely, as Lull galloped away.

See's gun hand lay at his thigh. "Talk all you like, but don't get restless with your hands. I'm telling you! Meddlesome? That's me. Matt is my middle name. Don't let that worry you any. I've got three good reasons for meddling. I know two of you, and I don't know the other one. I don't like waylaying— and I don't like you. Besides, I love to meddle. Always did. Everybody's business is my business. You three birds keep still and look sulky. Be wise, now! Me and a rattlesnake has got the same motto: You touch the button and I'll do the rest."

Black above and furnace flame below, the tumbling clouds came rushing from the hills with a mutter of far-off thunder. A glimmer of twilight lingered, and sudden stars blazed across the half sky to eastward, unclouded yet.

Hobby Lull cupped his hands and shouted through the dusk: "Hoo-e-ee!"

Johnny Dines halted the blue horse and answered blithely: "E-ee-hoo!"

"Sorry," said Lull as he rode up, "but I've got to put you under arrest."

"Anything serious?"

"Yes, it is. A man was killed back there to-day."

"So you want my gun, of course. Here it is. Don't mention it. I've had to hold strangers before now, myself."

"It isn't quite so vague as that—and I'm sorry, too," said Lull awkwardly. "This man was killed in Redgate Cañon and you came through there. I met you myself."

"Not that big red-headed chap I saw there?"

"That's the man."

"Hell, that's too bad. Acted like a good chap. He chinned with me a while—caught up with me and gave me a letter to mail. Where do we go—on or back? If you take

me to the John Cross wagon to-morrow they'll
tell you I'm all right.   Down on the river nobody seemed to know where the wagon was.
I'm Johnny Dines, Phillipsburg way. T-
Tumble-T brand."

"I've heard of you—no bad report either.
You live on one county line and I'm on the
other. Well, here's hoping you get safe out of
the mess. It isn't pretty. We'll take you on
to Hillsboro, I guess, now we're this close.
There's a lot more of us behind, waiting.
Let's go back and get them. Then we'll go
on."

"Look now—if you're going on to Hillsboro, my horse has come a right smart step to-
day, and every little bit helps. Why don't you
shoot a few lines? They'll come a-snuffin'
then, and we won't have to go back."

Hobby nodded.   He fired two shots.

"You ride a Bar Cross horse, I see."

"Yes. I'm the last hand." Johnny
grinned. "Hark! I hear them coming.
Sounds creepy, don't it? They're fussed.
Them two shots have got 'em guessing—
they're sure burning the breeze!   Say, I'm go-

ing to slip into my slicker.   Storm is right on top of us.   Getting mighty black overhead. Twilight lasts pretty quick in this country."

Rain spattered in big drops.   Wind-blown flare of stars and the last smoky dusk and flickers of lightning made a thin greenish light.   Shadowy horsemen shaped furiously through the murk, became clear, and reined beside them.   Dines took one look at them and directed a reproachful glance at his captor.

"I might not have handed over my gun so nice and easy if I had known who was with you," he remarked pleasantly.   A high spot of color flamed to his cheek.   "Just for that, you are going to lose the beauties of my conversation from now on—by advice of counsel. While you are putting on your slickers I merely wish to make a plain brief statement and also to call attention to one of the many mercies which crowd about us, and for which we are so ungrateful.   Mercies first: Did you ever notice how splendidly it has been arranged that one day follows directly after another, instead of in between?   And that maybe we're sometimes often quite sorry some day for what we did or didn't do some other day, or the reverse, as the case may be, or perhaps the contrary? Now the statement: I know two of you men, and I don't like those two; and for the others, I don't like the company they keep. So now you can all go to hell, home or Hillsboro, and take me with you, but I'll not entertain you, not if you was bored to death. I'm done and dumb—till I tell it to the judge."

X

"When the high heart we magnify
And the sure vision celebrate,
And worship greatness passing by—
Ourselves are great."
                    —JOHN DRINKWATER.

MR. GEORGE GWINNE sprawled at
his graceless ease along two chairs;
he held a long-stemmed brier-wood
pipe between his bearded lips and puffed
thoughtfully. The pipestem was long of
necessity; with a short stem Mr. Gwinne had
certainly set that beard alight. It was a
magnificent beard, such as you may not see
in these degenerate days. Nor did you see
many such in those degenerate days, for that
matter. It was long and thick and wide and
all that a beard should be; it reached from his
two big ears to below the fifth rib. It was
silky and wavy and curly, and—alas for poor
human nature!—it was kempt and kept—an
Assyrian beard. Yet Mr. George Gwinne
was, of all the sons of man, unlikeliest to be the
victim of vanity. His beard was a dusty red

brown, the thick poll of hair on his big square head was dusky red brown, lightly sprinkled with frost, his big eyes were reddish brown; and Argive Helen might have envied his brows, perfect brows in any other setting; merely comic here—no, no, "tragic" is the word, since all else about the man was coarse of grain and fiber, uncouth and repulsive.

His hands were big and awkward, and they swung from arms disproportionately long; his feet were big and flat, his body was big and gross, he was deep-chested and round-shouldered, his neck was a bull's neck, his ears were big and red, his head was big and coarse and square, his face was gnarled where it was not forested, his chance-seen lips were big and coarse, his nose was a monstrous beak, his voice was a hoarse deep rumble. And somewhere behind that rough husk dwelt a knightly soul, kindly and tender and sensitive —one of that glorious company, "who plotted to be worthy of the world."

He had friends—yes, and they held him high—but seeming and report held him pachyderm, and they trod upon his heart.

Only to a few have time and chance shown
a glimpse of the sad and lonely spirit behind
those tired eyes—and they have walked softlier
all their days for it. This is not his story; but
there will be a heavy reckoning when George
Gwinne's account goes to audit.

Mr. Gwinne's gaze rested benignantly on
a sleeping man; a young and smallish man,
very different from Mr. Gwinne in every respect, sprightly and debonair, even in sleep,
with careless grace in every line of him, just
as he had thrown himself upon the bunk. He
had removed hat and boots by way of preparation for bed, and his vest served for a pillow.
Long lashes lay on a cheek lightly tanned to
olive, but his upper forehead was startling
white by contrast, where a heavy hat had
shaded it from burning suns. His hands were
soft and white; the gloved hands of a rider in
his youth. The bunk, it may be mentioned,
was behind iron bars; Mr. Gwinne was chief
deputy and jailer, and the sleeper was Mr.
Johnny Dines.

Mr. Gwinne tapped out his pipe and spoke
huskily: "Young feller, get up! Can't you

hear the little birds singing their praises
to—"

"Ur-rgh! Ugh! Ar-rumph-umph!" said
Johnny, sitting up.

He started a little as his eyes fell on the
bars. He pulled his shoulders together.
Recollection followed puzzlement on his yet
unguarded face; he passed his fingers through
his tousled hair, making further tanglement.
He looked at the absurd gigantic figure beyond the bars, and his eyes crinkled to smiling.
Then his face took on an expression of discon-
tent. He eyed his bed with frank distaste.

"I say, old top—no offense, and all that,
but look now—I've never been in jail before.
Is the establishment all scientific and everything? No objectionable—er—creepers, you
know?"

"Why, you impudent young whelp! Damn
your hide, I sleep here myself. If there's a
grayback in my jail I'll eat your shirt. What
in time do you mean by it, hey? Pulling
my leg? You'd a heap better be studying
about your silly neck, you young devil. Come
out of that, now! Nine o'clock, past. Wish

I had your conscience.   Ten hours' solid sleep
and still going strong."

"Gee, why didn't you wake me up?   Are
they going to hold my preliminary trial this
morning or wait till after dinner?   I'm sort
of interested to see what indiscriminating evidence they've got."

"No trial to-day," said Gwinne gruffly.
"Justice of the peace is up in the hills beyond
Kingston, doin' assessments.   They've gone
after him, but they won't get back till late
to-night."

"H'm!" Johnny rubbed his nose and looked
searchingly at his ridiculously small and
shapely feet; he wriggled his toes.   "And
don't I eat till His Honor gets back?" he inquired diffidently.

Gwinne rose heavily and shambled to the
cell.   "If I let you out to eat breakfast with
me like a white man—no pranks?"

"Nary prank," said Johnny.

"She goes," said Gwinne.

He unlocked the door.   Johnny slipped on
his high-heeled boots and followed his jailer
to the kitchen.

"Water and washpan over there," said Gwinne, and poked fresh wood in the fire. "Ham and eggs this A. M." He rumbled a subterranean ditty:

Ham-fat, ham-fat, smoking in the pan—
There's a mighty sight of muscle on a ham-fat man.

Johnny sent an amused glance up and down his warden's inches.

"You must have been raised on it, then."

"Hog and hominy. There's a comb and brush."

"Got a comb." Johnny fumbled comb and toothbrush from his vest, and completed his toilet. "Haven't you had breakfast yet?"

"Naw. I hated to wake you up, you was hitting it off so regular. And you're the only prisoner I got now. Court's just over and the sheriff he's gone to Santa Fé with my only boarders. Lord only knows when he'll get back," said Mr. Gwinne parenthetically. "Jim is a good sheriff, a mighty good sheriff— but when he gets away from home he sees life through a glass darkly. They had him in jail, last time.   So I thought we might as well be sociable."

"Oh!   Then you're the party for me to jolly up when I want favors?"

"No," said Gwinne regretfully, "I'm not. The justice is gone, the sheriff's gone, and the district judge is always gone except when court sits here.   But the prosecuting attorney —he serves for the whole district, five counties, like the judge, you know—why, by bad luck, he's right here, a-hoppin' and a-rarin'.   So I'm under orders."

"Well, so am I.   What are they?   What can I do to help?"   The ham sizzled merrily. "Um-m!" said Johnny appreciatively.

"You might set the table.   I'll do the cooking to-day.   If so be you get to be a star boarder you'll have to do your share of the cooking—though I reckon they'll want me to keep you under key if you're bound over. Come to think, this prosecuting person would likely kick like a green bay horse if he knew I was lettin' you mill round foot-loose.   However, he don't know.   How many eggs? Hard or soft?"

"Oh, about four—medium. We can always cook more if we have to. And four pods of *chili*. But why has the prosecutor got it in for me? He don't want to cinch me unless I'm guilty, does he?"

"It isn't that, exactly. You see, it has got out that you ride for the Bar Cross. And the Bar Cross boys got Wade's goat, some way, down in Cruces. I don't know what they did, but he's sure on the peck, and here's where he stands to break even. Pour the coffee. Tin cow yonder on the shelf."

"Oh, well—he may have a little fun coming to him," said Johnny generously. "But let us hope, for his own sake, that he gives me a fair shake when it comes to my trial. If the Bar Cross and the John Cross aren't just satisfied they are capable of any rudeness—abandoned ruffians! Say, I hope someone took care of my Twilight horse."

"He's all right. I put him up with Otto Gans, myself. There, she's ready. *Sientese!*" The jailer seated himself opposite the guest. "No butter. You'll have to excuse me."

"Butter, hell. Whadya think I am—an incubator kid? Say, there's a few old vets here in Hillsboro that used to know my dad— me, too, when I was a little shaver, some of them. Spinal Maginnis, George Perrault, Kayler, Nick Galles and Preisser. H'm, let me see—and Jake Blun, Mabury and Page. Could you manage me a palaver with some one or two of 'em after breakfast?"

"Pleasure first, pain afterwards," growled Gwinne. "You eat a few lines while I hold high discourse to you about the good and great. District attorneys, now. Us being a territory thataway, district attorneys are appointed by the President—allee same like our judges and U. S. marshals and clerks of the court. All of 'em are appointed for four years, the same being the President's term. Presidents being so constituted by a wise and beneficent Providence, they appoint men from states where said men and their friends, if any, vote for President, and not from our humble midst. 'Cause why? We're not allowed to vote. More coffee?"

Johnny held his cup. Gwinne took up his discourse.

"Also, and moreover, they appoint politicians. We will not pursue this painful subject further except to add that, New Mexico being what and where it is, these appointees, while they might be first-class men and seldom were—they were always tenth-rate politicians. Because politicians rated higher than tenth-rate demanded something better. Yes. When Grover was in, they all came from Missouri, and they wasn't so bad but what they might have been worse, with proper care. And now they're all from darkest Injianny; a doubtful state. Something else, too. Even when they was well-meaning—which often was guessable—why, they're not our people. We have our little ways and they have their own little ways, and they're not the same little ways; and they rule us by their little ways. That's bad. To judge a man by the standards of another time and place is prejudging, and that means oppression, and oppression breeds riots in hell. That is how most trouble starts, I reckon—not understanding, prejudging. Men don't natu-

rally like to press down. They'd a heap
rather comfort and help—if they could just
see the way clear. Helping someone out of a
tight is just about the pleasantest thing a man
can do. But these people Uncle Sam sends
here to manage us, they don't think our
thoughts and they don't speak our tongue.
They ask for brick and we bring them mortar;
they ask for bread and we rock 'em to sleep.
That's the way I look at it. Won't you coin-
cide with me?"

"Why, yes," said Johnny, "now that you
mention it—I don't care if I do."

The jailer eyed his captive with painful dis-
trust. Then he sighed heavily.

"Flippant and inattentive! A bad mark.
Nine more demerits and you'll be suspended."
He rose and went to a closet and returned with
a bottle and glasses. "A long drop and a
quick finish!"

"Wishing you the same!" said Johnny
Dines. The glasses clinked together.

"So you be advised and don't waive examination," resumed Gwinne. "Wade will
want you to do that. Don't you listen to

Wade. You make your fight to-morrow. Old Andy Hinkle, the J. P., he's a homespun. When he hits a drill he hits her with all his carcass, from the ground up, and when he goes a-judging, justice is what he wants. His habit and disposition is real earnest and he mostly brings back what he goes after. You could rake all hell with a fine-tooth comb and not find a worse man to try you—if you killed Adam Forbes. If you did kill him you're goin' to lose your shadow soon—and there's your fortune told, right now."

"It is my thinking that I will make old bones yet, and tell tales in the chimney corner. Now you sit back and smoke while I wash up," said Johnny, gathering up the dishes. "I gotta ingratiate myself with you, you know. Go on, now—tell us some more. And how about me having a confidential with my friends?"

"That's just it. I was a-preparing of your mind, so you wouldn't be disappointed too much. This prosecuting person, Wade—he done instructed me not to let you see anyone except your lawyer."

"Lawyer, hell! What do I want of a lawyer?"

"Oh! Then you claim to be innocent, do you?" Gwinne's silken brows arched in assumed astonishment.

"Well, I hope so!" said Johnny indignantly. "If I was claiming to be guilty, why confab with my friends? Say, this is one raw deal if a fellow can't get an even break."

"Wade claims you might frame up something. He was particularly anxious the John Cross shouldn't hear of it until after your preliminary. Undue influence and all that."

"Frame up my foot! I didn't kill that man and I reckon I can prove it if I have any chance to know what evidence they're going to bring against me." Again that angry spot glowed on the clear olive of his cheek. "How can I study it over when I don't know what's happened or what is said to have happened? I'll have to go to trial in the dark—no chance to cipher on what's what, like I would if I had a chance to thresh it out with my friends."

"Well," said Gwinne gently, "what's the matter with me?"

"So that's all?" said Gwinne, after Dines had told his story. "Sure of it?"

"Absolutely. He rode up while I was branding my long-ear. He gave me a letter to mail and gassed while he smoked a cig, and wandered back the way he came, while I oozed away down the cañon. No more, no less. Said he was prospecting, he did—or did he?" Johnny reflected; remembering then that Forbes in giving him a letter to mail had mentioned location notices. "Yes, he did."

With the words another memory came into his mind, of the trouble with Jody Weir on day herd—about another letter, that was. This memory—so Johnny assured himself—flashed up now because Weir was one of his five accusers. No—there were only three accusers, as he understood it from the talk of the night before; three accusers, five to arrest him. Yet only one had come actually to make the arrest. Queer!

"Now," said Johnny, "it's your turn."

He curled a cigarette and listened. Early in the recital he rubbed his nose to stimulate thought; but later developments caused him

to transfer that attention to his neck, which
he stroked with caressing solicitude.   Once he
interrupted.

"I never stole a calf in a bare open hillside,
right beside a wagon road, never in my whole
life," he protested indignantly.   "As an ex-
perienced man, does that look reasonable to
you?"

"No, it don't," said Gwinne.   "But that's
the story.   Adam was found close by your fire
—shot in the back and dragged from the
stirrup; shot as he rode, so close up that his
shirt took fire.   And no one rode in Redgate
yesterday, but you, and those three, and Adam
Forbes."

"Yes.   That might very well be true," said
Johnny.

"It is true.   They wouldn't dare tell it that
way if it wasn't true.   Tracks show for themselves.   And they knew that good men would
be reading those tracks."

The prisoner rose and walked a little before
he made answer.   When he spoke at last it was
in a more serious tone.

"You see, I've got inside information.   I

know several things you don't know, that give
a different meaning to all this evidence and
all these tracks."

"Well," said Gwinne, "you need it. A
horse's track leads from the dead man to Garfield—a track that lacks one shoe."

"My horse had lost a shoe," said Johnny.

"Yes. You tacked one on him at Sam
Gray's store. But that is not the worst. The
worst is that there are three of them and only
one of you." Johnny felt of his neck again,
delicately. "By your tell there isn't any man
in the world to help out your bare word. If
you have any fresh dope, spill it."

"I happen to be in a position to state certainly, at first hand, something which modifies
the other evidence," said Dines slowly and
confidentially. "I happen to know positively
that I didn't murder that man. That's ex-
clusive. You only hear me say it—but I know
it. So you mustn't be hurt if I'm not convinced. If the horse tracks say I'm the
killer—the tracks are wrong, that's all. Or
wrongly read. You will be best served if you
either accept the full assurance of my guilt,

and so base your deductions on that, or else accept my innocence as sure, and read sign with that in mind.   It gets you nowhere to fit those tracks to both theories.   Such evidence will fit in with the truth to the last splinter, like two broken pieces of one stick.   It won't fit exactly with any lie, not the cleverest; there'll be a crack here, a splinter left over there, unaccountable.   For instance, if my accusers are right, the dead man's horse went down Redgate ahead of me; my tracks will be on top of his wherever we took the same trail."

"Exactly. That's what they say. They might have been mistaken. It is hard and stony ground."

"They may have been mistaken, yes. Someone else will see those tracks.   Now you listen close.   Listen hard.   If it turns out that Jody Weir and his two pardners, coming down Redgate on a run to give the alarm, rode over and rubbed out all tracks made by my horse and the dead man's horse, wherever they crossed each other—then that's another mistake they made.   For when I left Forbes there were only two fresh tracks in the cañon—

tracks of two fresh-shod horses going up the cañon, keeping to the road, and made yesterday. I'm sorry they didn't take me back to Garfield. I would have liked a peek at those tracks myself."

"But it rained, and it rained hard."

Johnny felt of his neck again.

"She sure did," he agreed. "Started just as this man Lull picked me, like fruit on the bough. I forgot that. Well, anyway, if this Garfield place is half human, then a slew of men went up Redgate Cañon before the rain. There must have been some live ones in the bunch."

"I wouldn't worry about that none if I was you," said the jailer. "I know Garfield, and I know old Pete Harkey, and he was taking the lead. If Adam's horse came down the cañon after you did, he'll know it. And if your track and the other were carefully ridden out where they crossed—why, old Pete will see that, too."

Johnny raised his hand. "That's what he will see! Hold that idea tight—squeeze it! If I am innocent, those tracks were ridden out and spoiled, till Adam Forbes' horse went one way and mine another."

"Well, then—Pete Harkey'll see that, too; he will think about it once and twice. Don't you worry. Jerome Martin and Jim-Ike-Jones went along, too, and old man Fenderson, maybe. They'll see. That's what they're going for."

"Hearsay evidence is no good in court. So I'm going to prophesy in writing—with you to witness and swear to the time of it—that all tracks this side of the murdered man are muddled. That written prophecy may not be evidence, but it will make the judge scratch his head."

"As much as to say—"

"Exactly. Someone killed Adam Forbes. You don't want to forget that. If it wasn't me—who was it? Well, let me tell you something. It was a mean man. Now you keep still a little, while I think over the meanest man I've seen lately."

Johnny rolled another smoke; and when it was alight he spoke again.

"Curious, when we come to think of it,

but the meanest things a man can do is what
he does with his mouth.   To kiss and tell, for
instance; betrayal under trust.   We go to
church and hear about the crucifixion.   We
have no hatred for the hands that drove the
nails or the soldier who stood guard—scarcely
for the fanatics who hounded the innocent to
a shameful death.   Our loathing is for Judas
Iscariot, who betrayed with a kiss."

Gwinne eyed his captive benevolently.

"Good land of Goshen, son—what on earth
has all this got to do with the price of hemp?"

"Everything to do with it.   Demand for
hemp is going to fluctuate violently if I can
swing the deal I have in mind," replied
Johnny, with spirit.   "I was just thinking
about two traitors I know."

In a prolonged silence Mr. Gwinne rum-
pled his beard and refilled his pipe.

"The two Garfield men and the other three
did not seem to be agreeing very well," he said
at last.   "Lull—he's the one who arrested you
—he went back to Garfield last night.
Couldn't sleep, he said, and they'd be wanting
to know in Garfield.   The other one, See, the

least one, he was round here soon this morning wanting to talk it up with you.   He was real feverish about the quarantine."

Johnny cocked his head impishly and looked sidelong at the jailer.

"Just what was the big idea for sending one man to arrest me?"

"They didn't say."

"And why were they all crosswise with each other, like jackstraws?"

"They didn't tell me that either."

"You're allowed three guesses."

Gwinne puffed unhurriedly at his pipe, and after some meditation delivered himself of a leisurely statement between puffs.

"About a year ago, near as I can remember, this man Caney—Big Ed Caney—deputy sheriff in Dona Ana—did you know that? Thought not.   Well, he went out beyond Hatch with a warrant for a fellow.   He found another man—old Mexican sheep herder—cut down on him with a rifle and ordered him to throw 'em up.   The old Mexican was scared or else he remembered something, I don't know which; he was perfectly innocent of this particular charge, whatever it was; they caught the other man later. Anyhow the old gentleman made a dash for his gun—it was leaning up against a tree not far away. And Caney killed him."

"So you think maybe Caney wanted to start something. Ambush, maybe? So I'd go after my gun?"

"I don't know anything about what Caney wanted to do or didn't want to do. All I know is—he didn't."

"And the Garfield boys wouldn't stand for it?" persisted Johnny.

"Lull and Charlie See won't stand for any crooked work—if it's them you mean. Lull was the only Garfield man. Charlie See is from Dona Ana, where they grow good and bad, same as they do here."

"Yes. I see. I know Jody and Toad Hales, myself. I met Lull and See yesterday evenin', just out of Garfield. Say, Mr. Gwinne, could you rustle me a razor?"

"I can too. Anything else on your mind?"

"Why, no. Only I wish I knew where the

John Cross outfit is holding forth, and when they are likely to get word about me being in a tight. They may hear to-day, and it may be a week."

"They're up beyond Hermosa, somewhere at the head of Cuchillo Creek. And I shouldn't much wonder if they heard about you to-day sometime." Mr. Gwinne looked through the window at the visible wedge of Hillsboro, wavy low hills and winding streets; looked with long and lingering interest, and added irrelevantly: "I knew your father."

Late that afternoon a heavy knock came at the outer door of the jail. Gwinne hustled his prisoner into a cell and answered the call.

He was greeted at the door by Aloys Preisser, the assayer, a gay-hearted old Bavarian— the same for whom, in his youth, Preisser Hill was named—and by Hobby Lull. Hobby's face was haggard and drawn; there were dark circles under his eyes.

"We want to settle a bet," announced Hobby, "and we're leaving it to you. I say

that Robin Hood knocked out the Proud
Sheriff of Nottingham, and Preisser claims it
was a draw. How about it?"

"Hood got the decision on points," said
Gwinne soberly.

"There! What did I tell you, you old hunk
of Limburger?" Hobby Lull laid hands
delicately upon his adversary's short gray
beard and tugged it with deferential gentleness. The unresisting head wagged sedately
to and fro. "Take that, you old bug hunter!"
said Hobby, and stood back, waiting.

The assayer became statuesque.

"You see, Mister Deputy? He has assauldt
gommitted, and you a witness are. With
abusive language!"

"The wienerwurst is yet to come," observed
Lull, in a voice sepulchral and ominous.

"With threats also, and insults—abandoned
ruffian! Desperate! Catiline! Officer—do
your duty! I make demand of you. Dake
dot mon into gustody!" Preisser's eyes were
dancing as he fought down a grin.

Mr. Gwinne regarded the impassioned dis-
putants with grave eyes.

"You are under arrest, Mr. Lull," he said with somber official severity. "Can you give bail?"

"Not one red cent."

"Come in, then."

Lull followed through the door. Turning, he smiled back at the little assayer. Preisser winked.

"I'll have to lock you up, you know," said Gwinne. "District attorney particularly desired that no one should hold communication with Dines, over yonder." He locked Lull in a cell; forgetfully leaving the key in the lock. "Don't try to shout across to Dines, now," he warned. "I'll hear you. Well, I'll be meanderin' along to the kitchen and starting supper."

Hobby reached through the bars and turned the key. He went over to Johnny's cell.

"Well, Dines, how goes it? You don't look much downhearted."

"I'm not," said Johnny. "I'm sorry about the dead man, of course. But I didn't know him, and you can't expect me to feel like you do. I'm right as rain—but I can't say as much for you. You look like you'd been dragged through a knothole."

"No sleep. I went back to Garfield, made medicine, and hurried back here. Seventy-five miles now, after a day's work and not much sleep the night before. I thought you'd be having your prelim, you see, or I'd have waited over. Didn't know that Judge Hinkle was out of town."

"Any news?"

"Yes," said Hobby, "there is."

He held out his hand. Johnny took it, through the bars.

"You don't think I killed your friend, then?"

"I know you didn't. But, man—we can't prove it. Not one scrap of evidence to bring into court. Just a sensing and a hunch—against a plain, straight, reasonable story, with three witnesses. You are It."

"Now you can't sometimes most always ever tell," said Johnny. "Besides, you're tired out. Get you a chair and tell it to me. I've been asleep. Also, you and I have had some few experiences not in common before our trails crossed yesterday. I may do a little sensing myself. Tell it to me."

"Well, after Caney's crowd told us Adam was killed in Redgate, Uncle Pete and a bunch went up there hotfoot. They found everything just about as Caney told it. There was your track, with one shoe gone, and Adam's horse with the bridle dragging—till he broke it off—"

"And where those two tracks crossed," interrupted Johnny, "those fellows had ridden over the trail till you couldn't tell which was on top."

Hobby stared.

"How did you know that? Uncle Pete was all worked up over it. I never heard him so powerful before, on any subject."

"You're tired out, so you can't see straight," said Johnny. "Also, I know that when I came down Redgate there were no fresh tracks heading this way. If those three men killed Forbes and want to saw it off on me—then they confused that trail on purpose. If they didn't kill Forbes, and muddled the tracks that way, they're half-wits. And they're not half-wits. Go on."

"They found poor old Adam and your fire. They pushed on ahead to read all the sign they could before dark. Up in the park there'd been a heap of riding back and forth. Just at dark they found where a bunch of cattle had been headed and had gone over the divide into Deadman and gone on down. Then the rain came—and the rest is mud."

"Yes. It rained. There was a little low gap to the north from where I branded my calf. If anybody had been there making tracks—those cattle would blot 'em out." Johnny began to laugh. "Look, *amigo*—all this dope seems fairly reasonable and night-mareish, turn about, as we see it across thirty miles and twenty-four hours—but it is a safe guess that some folks didn't sleep much last night. They know all about it, and I reckon when they got to thinking it over it seemed to them like the whole story was printed in letters a mile high. Scared? I guess yes. I'd hate to trade places with 'em right now. And before it rained—oh, mamma! I bet they was tickled to see that rain! Well, go on. Proceed. Give us some more."

"The further I go the less you'll like it," said Lull. "Pete and his hand-picked posse stayed up there and scattered out at daylight, for general results. They found one of Adam's cows with a big fresh-branded calf—branded yesterday. Dines, you're up against it—hard! It's going to look black to any jury. That calf carried your brand—T-Tumble-T!"

"'Hellfire and damnation—make my bed soon!'" said Johnny. "The boy stood on the burning deck, With neither high nor low! The Sons of Zeruiah! . . . Ho, warder! Pull up the drawstring! Let the portcrayon fall! Melt down the largess, fling out the pendulum to the breeze, and howl the battle cry of Dines!"

Hobby's gaunt features relaxed to a laugh.

"You silly ass! And the rope on your very neck! And what is the battle cry of Dines, if I may ask?"

"Only two out!" said Johnny Dines. He

flung up his head; his hawk's face was beautiful.

"Good boy!" said Hobby Lull. "Good boy! You never shot Adam Forbes—not in the back. You hold your mouth right. It isn't so bad, Dines. I wanted to see how you'd take it. I know you now. There's more to come. You live a long way from here, with roughs and the river between. We've never seen any of your cattle. But we looked you up in the brand book. Your earmark is sharp the right, underslope the left. That yearling's ears are marked sharp the left, underslope the right."

"Yes. And I knew that without looking at the brand book," said Johnny. "They've overplayed their hand. Any more?"

"One thing more. Nothing to put before a jury—but it fits with a frame-up. This morning, Uncle Pete scouted round beyond where they quit the trail at dark. He found locations where Weir and Caney and Hales struck rich placer yesterday. A big thing—coarse gold. It was natural enough that they didn't tell us. For that matter, they men-

tioned prospecting along with their saddle-
thieves' hunt. You heard 'em tell Gwinne
about the saddle thieves last night. But—
Adam Forbes was prospecting too. That's
what he went up there for. Caney, Weir and
Hales—any one of them has just the face of a
man to turn lead into gold. There's a motive
for you—a possible motive."

"More than possible. Let me think!"
Johnny nursed his knee. He saw again the
cool dark windings of Redgate, the little
branding fire, the brushy pass low above
him—where a foe might lurk—himself and
Forbes, clear outlined on the hillside, the
letter Forbes had given him.

"H'm!" he said. "H'm! Exactly!" With
a thoughtful face, he chanted a merry little
stave:

> *The soapweed rules over the plain,*
> *And the brakeman is lord of the train,*
> *The prairie dog kneels*
> *On the back of his heels,*
> *Still patiently praying for rain.*

"Say, Mr. Lull, isn't it a queer lay to have

the county seat inland, not on the railroad at
all, like Hillsboro?"

"That's easy.   Hillsboro was the county seat
before there was any railroad."

"Oh—that way?   And how do you get your
mail at Garfield?   Does that come from
Hillsboro?"

"No.   Hillsboro is the closest post office,
but our mail goes to Rincon.   There's the
river, you see, and no bridge.   A letter takes
two days and a hundred miles to get from
Garfield to Hillsboro—and it's only twenty-
five miles straight across in low water."

"I see," said Johnny.

Again he visioned the scene on the hillside,
the fire, Adam Forbes, the location papers he
was to mail; he remembered Toad Hales and
his attempted betrayal of the horse-camp
guest; he remembered Jody Weir's letter to
Hillsboro, and how it was to be delivered.
Jody Weir—and the girl in Hillsboro post
office—steady, Johnny—steady, boy!   Even
so, Jody Weir could keep those location papers
from reaching the recorder!

The whole black business became clear and

sure to him. And in that same flaming moment he knew that he could not clear himself by shaming this light lady—that he had never seen or known. To shield her fault or folly, he must take his chance. He looked up and spread out his hands.

"No go, Mr. Lull!" he said cheerfully. "Much obliged to you—and here is gear enough for a cuckoo clock, but I can't make it tick. Surmise and suspicion. Not one fact to lay hands on. Something may come out in the trial, of course. Looks like both ends against the middle, don't it? When dry weather keeps you poor and a rain hangs you? Tough luck! Alas, poor Johnny! I knew him well!"

So far his iron fortunes had brought him— to the shadow of the gallows. There, beset with death and shame, with neck and name on the venture, he held his head high, and kept his honor spotless. Well done, Johnny Dines! Well played, our side!

There is somewhat which must be said here. Doubtless it is bad Art—whatever that means

—but it is a thing to be done. It is charged to me that I suppress certain sorry and unsavory truths when I put remembered faces to paper—that I pick the best at their best, and shield with silence their hours of shame and weakness—these men I loved. Well—it is true. I take my own risk by that; but for them, it is what they have deserved. It is what Johnny Dines did for Kitty Seiber.

"Well, that's about all," said Hobby. "Uncle Pete is still skirmishing round. Adam had a tame tank somewhere close by, and Pete thinks he may find some more light on the case, there or somewheres else. If you don't think of anything more I guess I'll go down to the Gans Hotel and sleep a day or two. Nobody knows where See is. He may be asleep—and then again he may be up to some devilment."

"From what I could hear a while ago," said Johnny, grinning hugely, "I thought you were a prisoner."

"I am," said Hobby.

He went to a window at the end of the

big hall and looked out. Hillsboro is generously planned, and spreads luxuriously over more hills than Rome. This is for two reasons: First, there was plenty of room, no need to crowd; second, and with more of the causative element, those hills were rich in mineral, and were dotted thick with shaft and tunnel between the scattered homes.

Several shafts were near the jail. On the nearest one Mr. Preisser diligently examined the ore dump. Hobby whistled. Mr. Preisser looked up. Hobby waved his hat. Preisser waved back and started toward the jail. Hobby returned to his cell and locked himself in. Mr. Preisser thundered at the jail door.

"Well?" said Gwinne, answering the summons.

"I have been thinking about the criminal, Lull," said Mr. Preisser, beaming. "Considering his tender years and that he is nod fully gompetent and responsible mentally—I have decided nod to bress the charge against him. You may let him go, now."

"Oh, very well," said Gwinne.

He went to the cell—without remark concerning the key in the lock—and set the prisoner free. His face kept a heavy seriousness; there was no twinkle in his eye. Assailant and victim went arm in arm down the hill.

Mr. Charlie See came softly to Hillsboro jail through the velvet night. He did not come the front way; he came over the hill after a wearisome detour. He approached the building on the blind side, cautiously as any cat, and crouched to listen in the shadow of the wall. After a little he began a slow voyage of discovery. At the rear of the building a broad shaft of light swept out across the hill. This was the kitchen. See heard Gwinne's heavy tread, and the cheerful splutterings of beefsteak. Then he heard a dog within; a dog that scratched at the door with mutter and whine.

"Down, Diogenes!" growled Gwinne; and raised his voice in a roaring chorus:

> *"And he sunk her in the lonesome lowland low—*
> *And he sunk her in the lowland sea!"*

Charlie retraced his steps to the corner and the friendly shadows. He crept down the long blank side of the jail, pausing from time to time to listen; hearing nothing. He turned the corner to the other end. A dim light showed from an unwindowed grating. The investigator stood on a slope and the window place was high. Reaching up at full stretch, he seized the bars with both hands, stepped his foot on an uneven stone of the foundation, and so pulled himself up to peer in—and found himself nose to nose with Johnny Dines.

The prisoner regarded his visitor without surprise.

"Good evening," he observed politely.

"Good eve— Oh, hell! Say, I ought to bite your nose off—you and your good evening! Look here, fellow—are you loose in there?"

"Oh, yes. But the outer door's locked."

"Well, by gracious, you'd better be getting to thunder out of this! You haven't a chance. You're a gone goose. You ought to hear the talk I've heard round town.

They're going to hang you by the neck!"

"Well, why not—if I did that?" inquired Johnny, reasonably enough. They spoke in subdued undertones.

"But I know damn well you didn't do it."

The rescuer spoke with some irritation; he was still startled. Johnny shook his head thoughtfully.

"The evidence was pretty strong—what I heard of it, anyhow."

"I guess, by heck, I know a frame-up when I see it. Say, what the hell are you talking about? You wild ass of the desert! Think I got nothing to do but hang on here by my eyelashes and argue with you? One more break like that and down goes your meat house—infernal fool! Listen! There's a mining shaft right over here—windlass with a ratchet wheel and a pawl. I can hook that windlass rope on these bars and yank 'em out in a jiffy. If the bars are too stubborn I'll strain the rope tight as ever I can and then pour water on it. That'll fetch 'em; won't make much noise, either, I judge. Not now— your jailer man will be calling you to supper in a minute. Maybe we'd better wait till he goes to sleep—or will he lock you up? Fellow, what you want to do is go. You can make Old Mexico to-morrow. I'll side you if you say so. I've got nothing to keep me here."

"Now ain't that too bad—and I always wanted to go to Mexico, too," said Johnny wistfully. "But I reckon I can't make it this riffle. You see, this old rooster has treated me pretty white—not locked me up, and everything. I wouldn't like to take advantage of it. Come to think of it, I told him I wouldn't."

"Well, say!" Charlie stopped, at loss for words. "I get your idea—but man, they'll hang you!"

"I'm sorry for that, too," said Johnny regretfully. "But you see how it is. I haven't any choice. Much obliged, just the same." Then his face brightened. "Wait! Wait a minute. Let me think. Look now—if Gwinne locks me up in a cell, bimeby—why, you might come round and have another try, later on. That will be different."

"I'll go you once on that," returned the rescuer eagerly. "Which is your cell?"

"Why, under the circumstances it wouldn't be just right to tell you—would it, now?" said the prisoner, doubtfully. "I reckon you'll have to project round and find that out for yourself."

"Huh!" snorted Charlie See.

"Of course if I make a get-away it looks bad—like admitting the murder. On the other hand, if I'm hanged, my friends would always hate it. So there we are. On the whole, I judge it would be best to go. Say, Gwinne'll be calling me to chuck. Reckon I better beat him to it. You run on, now, and roll your hoop. I'll be thinking it over. G'night!"

His face disappeared from the embrasure. Charlie See retired Indian-fashion to the nearest cover, straightened up, and wandered discontentedly down the hill to Hillsboro's great white way.

XI

"We retired to a strategic position prepared in advance."
—*Communiqués of the Crown Prince.*

CHARLIE SEE was little known in the county seat. It was not his county, to begin with, and his orbit met Hillsboro's only at the intersection of their planes. Hillsboro was a mining town, first, last and at all intervening periods. Hillsboro's "seaport," Lake Valley, was the cowman's town; skyward terminus of the High Line, twig from a branch railroad which was itself a feeder for an inconsiderable spur. The great tides of traffic surged far to north and south. This was a remote and sheltered backwater, and Hillsboro lay yet twelve miles inland from Lake Valley. Here, if anywhere, you found peace and quiet; Hillsboro was as far from the tumult and hurly-burly as a corner of Fifth Avenue and Forty-second Street.

Along the winding way, where lights of business glowed warm and mellow, feverish knots and clusters of men made a low-voiced

237

buzzing; a buzzing which at See's approach
either ceased or grew suddenly clear to discussion of crossroads trivialities. From one
of these confidential knots, before the Gans
Hotel, a unit detached itself and strolled down
the street.

"Howdy, Mr. See," said the unit as Charlie
overtook it. "Which way now?"

"Oh, just going round to the hardware store
to get a collar button."

"You don't know me," said the sauntering
unit. "My name is Maginnis."

"I withdraw the collar button," said
Charlie. He slowed his step and shot a
glance at the grizzled face beside him.
Who's Who in Cowland has a well-thumbed
page for Spinal Maginnis. "What's your
will?"

"You arrested young Dines?"

"In a way, yes. I was with the bunch."

"It is told of you by camp fires," said
Maginnis, "that you'll do to take along. Will
you come?"

"With you, yes. Spill it."

"For me. To do what I can't do for my-

self.   You arrested Johnny Dines, or helped;
so you can go where I'm not wanted.   Notice
anything back yonder?"   He jerked his head
toward the main street.

"Well, I'm not walking in my sleep this
bright beautiful evening.   Whispering fools,
you mean?"

"Exactly.   Some knaves, too.   But fools
are worse always, and more dangerous.   This
town is all fussed up and hectic about the
Forbes killing.   Ugly rumors—Dines did
this, Dines did that, Dines is a red hellion.   I
don't like the way things shape up.   There's a
lot of offscourings and riffraff here—and
someone is putting up free whisky.   It's
known that I was a friend of this boy's father,
and it is suspected that I may be interested in
his father's son.   But you—can't you find out
—Oh, hell, you know what I want!"

"Sure I do.   You're afraid of a mob, with
a scoundrel back of it.   Excuse me for wasting
words.   You're afraid of a mob.   I'm your
man.   Free whisky is where I live.   Me for
the gilded haunts of sin.   Any particular
haunt you have in mind?"

"Sure I have. No need to go to The Bank. Joe is a pretty decent old scout. You skip Joe's place and drop in at The Mermaid. Where they love money most is where trouble starts."

"Where will I report to you?"

"You know Perrault's house?"

"With trees all round, and a little vineyard? Just below the jail? Yes."

"You'll find me there, and a couple more old residenters. Hop along, now."

The Mermaid saloon squatted in a low, dark corner of Hillsboro—even if the words were used in the most literal sense.

Waywardly careless, Hillsboro checkered with alternate homes and mines the undulations of a dozen low hills; an amphitheater girdled by high mountain walls, with a central arena for commercial gladiators. Stamp mills hung along the scarred hillsides, stamp mills exhibiting every known variety of size and battery. In quite the Athenian manner, courthouse, church and school crowned each a hill of its own, and doubtless proved what has been so often and so well said of our civi-

lization. At any rate the courthouse cost
more than the school—about as much more as
it was used less; and the church steeple was
such as to attract comment from any god.
The school was less imposing.

This was a high, rainy country. The frontier of the pines lay just behind and just above
the town, on the first upward slopes. The
desert levels were far below. Shade trees,
then, can grow in Hillsboro; do grow there by
Nature and by artifice, making a joyous riot
of visible song—in the residential section.
Industrial Hillsboro, however, held—or was
held?—to the flintier hills, bleak and bare and
brown, where the big smelter overhung and
dominated the north. The steep narrow valley of the Percha divided Hillsboro rather
equally between the good and the goats.

There was also the inevitable Mexican quarter—here, as ever, Chihuahua. But if Hillsboro could claim no originality of naming,
she could boast of something unique in map
making. The Mexican suburb ran directly
through the heart of the town. Then the
Mexican town was the old town? A good

guess, but not the right one. The effective cause was that the lordly white man scorned to garden—cowmen and miners holding an equally foolish tradition on this head; while the humble *paisano* has gardened since Scipio and Hasdrubal; would garden in hell. So the narrow bottom lands of the creek were given over to truck patches and brown gardeners; tiny empires between loop and loop of twisting water; black loam, pay dirt. It is curious to consider that this pay dirt will be fruitful still, these homes will still be homes, a thousand years after the last yellow dross has been sifted from the hills.

So much for the town proper. A small outlying fringe lay below the broad white wagon road twisting away between the hills in long curves or terraced zigzags to the railhead. Here a flat black level of glassy obsidian shouldered across the valley and forced the little river to an unexpected whirling plunge where the dark box of the Percha led wandering through the eastern barrier of hills; and on that black cheerless level huddled the wide, low length of The Mermaid, paintless, forbidding, shunning and shunned. Most odd to contemplate; this glassy barren, nonproducing, uncultivated and unmined, waste and sterile, was yet a better money-maker than the best placer or the richest loam land of all Hillsboro. Tellurian papers please copy.

The Mermaid boasted no Jonson, and differed in other respects from The Mermaid of Broad Street. Nor might it be reproached with any insidious allure, though one of the seven deadly arts had been invoked. Facing the bar, a startled sea maid turned her head, ever about to plunge to the safety of green seas. The result was not convincing; she did not look startled enough to dive. But perhaps the artist had a model. Legend says the canvas was painted to liquidate a liquor bill, which would explain much; it is hard paying for a dead horse. It had once been signed, but some kindly hand had scraped the name away. In moments of irritation Hillsboro spoke of The Mermaid as "The Dive."

"Johnny Dines—yah! Thought he could pull that stuff and get away with it," said Jody Weir loudly. "Fine bluff, but it got called.

Bankin' on the cowmen to stick with him and get him out of it."

The Mermaid bar was crowded. It was a dingy place and a dingy crew. The barkeeper had need for all his craft and swiftness to give service. The barkeeper was also the owner—a tall man with a white bloodless face, whiter for black brows like scars. The gambling hall behind was lit up but deserted. The crowd was in too ugly a mood for gambling. They had been drinking bad liquor, much too much for most of them; headed by Weir, Caney and Hales, seconded by any chance buyer, and followed up by the Merman, who served a round on the house with unwonted frequency.

Jody pounded on the bar.

"Yes, that's his little scheme—intimidation. He's countin' on the cowboys to scare Hillsboro out—him playin' plumb innocent of course—knowin' nothin', victim of circumstances. Sure! 'Turn this poor persecuted boy loose!' they'll say. 'You got nothin' on him.' Oh, them bold bad men!"

"That don't sound reasonable, Jody," objected Shaky Akins. "Forbes was a cowman. You're a cowman yourself."

"Yes—but I saw. These fellers'll hear, and then they'll shoot off their mouths on general principles, not knowing straight up about it; then they'll stick to what they first said, out of plumb pig-headedness. One thing I'm glad of: I sure hope Cole Ralston likes the way his new man turned out."

"Dines and Charlie See favor each other a heap. Not in looks so much," said Shaky, "but in their ways. I used to know Charlie See right well, over on the Pecos. He was shortstop on the Roswell nine. He couldn't hit, and he couldn't field, and he couldn't run bases—but oh, people, how that man could play ball!"

"Nonsense. They're not a bit alike. You think so, just because they're both little."

"I don't either. I think so because they're both—oh my!"

"I don't like this man See, either," said Caney. "I don't like a hair of his head. Too damn smart. Somebody's going to break him in two before he's much older."

"Now listen!" said Shaky Akins, without heat. "When you go to break Charlie See you'll find he is a right flexible citizen—any man, any time, anywhere."

"Well," said Hales, "all this talking is dry work. Come up, boys. This one is on me."

"What will it be, gentlemen?" inquired the suave Merman. "One Scotch. Yes. Three straights. A highball. Three rums. One gin sling. Make it two? Right. Next? Whisky straight. And the same. What's yours, Mr. Akins?"

"Another blond bland blend," said Shaky. "But you haven't answered my question, Jody. Why should cowmen see this killing any different from anyone else? Just clannishness, you think?"

"Because cowmen can read sign," said Charlie See. He stood framed in the front door: he stepped inside.

The startled room turned to the door. There were nudges and whispers. Talking ceased. There had been a dozen noisy conversations besides the one recorded.

"Reading tracks is harder to learn than Greek, and more interesting," said Charlie. "Cattlemen have always had to read sign, and they've always had to read it right—ever since they was six years old. What you begin learning at six years old is the only thing you ever learn good. So cowmen don't just look and talk. They see and think."

He moved easily across the room in a vast silence. Caney's eyes met those of the Merman barkeeper. The Merman's bloodless and sinister face made no change, but he made a change in the order.

"Step up, Mr. See," said the Merman. "This one's on me. What will it be?"

"Beer," said Charlie. He nodded to the crowd. "Howdy, boys! Hello, Shaky—that you?"

He lined up beside Shaky; he noted sly sidelong glances and furtive faces reflected in the blistered mirror behind the bar.

"Sure is. Play you a game of pool—what?"

"All set?" demanded Caney from the other

end of the bar. "Drink her down, fellers! Here's to the gallows tree!"

"Looks like a good season for fruit," said Charlie. A miner laughed.

Shaky drained his glass. "Come on, pool shark." He hooked his arm in Charlie's and they went back to the big hall. Part of the crowd drifted after them.

There was only one pool table, just beyond the door. Down one side were ranged tables for monte, faro, senate and stud. On the other side the bar extended beyond the partition and took up twenty feet of the hall, opposite the pool table. On the end of the bar were ranged generous platters of free lunch—shrimps, pretzels, strips of toasted bread, sausages, mustard, pickles, olives, crackers and cheese. Behind it was a large quick-lunch oil stove, darkened now. Beyond that was a vast oak refrigerator with a high ornamental top reaching almost to the ceiling. Next in order was a crap table and another for seven-and-a-half. A big heater, unused now, shared the central space with the pool table. Between these last two was a small table littered with papers and magazines. Two or three men sat there reading.

"Pretty quiet to-night?" said Charlie, nodding his chin at the sheeted games.

"Yes. Halfway between pay days. Don't pay to start up," said Shaky carelessly. "At that, it is quieter than usual to-night."

They played golf pool.

"It is not true that everyone who plays golf pool goes goopy," remarked Charlie at the end of the first game. "All crazy men play golf pool, of course. But that is not quite the same thing, I hope. Beware of hasty deductions—as the bank examiner told the cashier. Let's play rotation."

Jody Weir stuck his head through the doorway. "Hey, you! I'm buying. Come have a drink!"

Most of the loungers rose and went forward to the bar. The men at the reading table did not move; possibly they did not hear. One was an Australian, a simple-faced giant, fathoms deep in a Sydney paper; his lips moved as he read, his eye glistened.

"Let's go up to the hotel," said Akins.

"This table is no good.   They got a jim dandy up there.   New one."

"Oh, this is all right," said Charlie.   "I'll break.   Say, Shaky, you've seen my new ranch.   What'll you give me for it, lock, stock and barrel, lease, cattle and cat, just as she lays, everything except the saddle stock?   I'm thinking some about drifting."

"That's a good idea—a fine idea," said Shaky.   He caught Charlie's eye, and pointed his brows significantly toward the barroom. "Where to?"

"Away.   Old Mex, I guess.   Gimme a bid."

Shaky considered while he chalked his cue. Then he shook his head.

"No.   Nice place—but I wouldn't ever be satisfied there. . . . Mescaleros held up a wagon train there in 1879—where your pasture is now, halfway between your well and Mason's Ranch.   Killed thirteen men and one woman.   I was a kid then, living at Fort Selden.   A damn fool took me out with the burial party, and I saw all those mutilated

bodies. I never got over it. That's why I'm
Shaky Akins."

"Why, I thought—" began See uncomfort-
ably.

"No. 'Twasn't chills. I'm giving it to
you straight. I hesitated about telling you.
I've never told anyone—but there's a reason
for telling you—now—to-night. I lost my
nerve. I'm not a man. See, I've dreamed
of those people ten thousand times. It's hell!"

Weir's head appeared at the door again;
his face was red and hot.

"You, See! Ain't you comin' out to
drink?"

"Why, no. We're playing pool."

"Well, I must say, you're not a bit—"

"I know I'm not a bit," said See placidly.
"That's no news. I've been told before that
I'm not a bit. You run on, now. We're play-
ing pool."

The face withdrew. There was a hush in
the boisterous mirth without. Then it rose in
redoubled volume.

"Come up to the hotel with me," urged

Shaky, moistening his lips. "I got a date with a man there at ten. We can play pool there while I'm waiting."

"Oh, I'll stay here, I guess. I want to read the papers."

"You headstrong little fool," whispered Akins. "Their hearts is bad—can't you see? Come along!" Aloud he said: "If you get that ball it makes you pool."

The door from the barroom opened and two men appeared. One, a heavy man with a bullet head much too small for him, went to the free lunch; the other, a dwarfish creature with a twisted sullen face, walked to the Australian and shook him by the shoulder.

"Come on, Sanders. Say good night to the library. You're a married man and you don't want to be in this." His voice had been contemptuously kind so far; but now he snarled hatred. "Hell will be popping here pretty quick, and some smart Aleck is going to get what's coming to him. Oh, bring your precious 'pyper,' if you want to. Sim won't mind. Come along—Larriken!"

The big man followed obediently.

"Part of that is good," observed **Shaky** Akins. "The part where he said good night. I'm saying it."

He made for the back door. The other man at the reading table rose and followed him.

"Good night, Shaky.   Drop me a post hole, sometime," said Charlie.

The bullet-head man, now eating toast and shrimps, regarded See with a malicious sneer. See rummaged through the papers, selected a copy of The Black Range, and seated himself sidewise on the end of the billiard table; then laying the paper down he reached for the triangle and pyramided the pool balls.

The swinging door crashed inward before a vicious kick.   Caney stalked in.   His pitted face was black with rage.   Weir followed. As the door swung to there was a glimpse of savage eager faces crowded beyond.

Caney glared across the billiard table.

"We're not good enough for you to drink with, I reckon," he croaked.

Charlie laid aside the triangle.   The free

lunch man laughed spitefully. "Aren't you?" said Charlie, indifferently.

Caney raised his voice. "And I hear you been saying I was a gallows bird?"

Charlie See adjusted a ball at the corner of the pyramid. Then he gave to Caney a slow and speculative glance.

"Now that I take a good look at you—it seems probable, don't it?"

"Damn you!" roared Caney. "What do you mean?"

"Business!"

No man's eye could have said which hand moved first. But See was the quicker. As Caney's gun flashed, a pool ball struck him over the heart, he dropped like a log, his bullet went wide. A green ball glanced from Jody's gun arm as it rose; the cartridge exploded harmlessly as the gun dropped; Weir staggered back, howling. He struck the swinging door simultaneously with the free-lunch man; and in that same second a battering-ram mob crashed against it from the other side. Weir was knocked sprawling; the door sagged from a broken hinge. See crouched

behind the heavy table and pitched. Two
things happened. Bullets plowed the green
cloth of the table and ricocheted from the
smooth slate; bushels of billiard balls streamed
through· the open door and thudded on
quivering flesh. Flesh did not like that. It
squeaked and turned and fled, tramping the
fallen, screaming. Billiard balls crashed
sickeningly on defenseless backs. In cold
fact, Charlie See threw six balls; at that
close range flesh could have sworn to sixty.
Charlie felt rather than saw a bloodless face
rise behind the bar; he ducked to the shelter
of the billiard table as a bullet grooved the
rail; his own gun roared, a heavy mirror
splintered behind the bar: the Merman had
also ducked. Charlie threw two shots through
the partition. At the front, woodwork
groaned and shattered as a six-foot mob passed
through a four-foot door. Charlie had a
glimpse of the crouching Merman, the last
man through. For encouragement another
shot, purposely high, crashed through the tran-
som; the Merman escaped in a shower of glass.

"How's that, umpire?" said Charlie See.

The business had been transacted in ten seconds. If one man can cover a hundred yards in ten seconds how many yards can forty men make in the same time?

"Curious!" said Charlie. "Some of that bunch might have stood up to a gun well enough. But they can't see bullets. And once they turned tail—good night!"

He slipped along the rail to the other end of the table, his gun poised and ready. Caney sprawled on the floor in a huddle. His mouth was open, gasping, his eyes rolled back so that only the whites were visible, his livid face twitched horribly. See swooped down on Caney's gun and made swift inspection of the cylinder; he did the like by Weir's, and then tiptoed to· the partition door, first thrusting his own gun into his waistband. The barroom was empty; only the diving Mermaid smiled invitation to him. See turned and raced for the back door. Even as he turned a gust of wind puffed through the open front door and the wrecked middle door; the lamps flared, the back door slammed with a crash.

With the sound of that slamming door, a

swift new thought came to See. He checked, halted, turned back. He took one look at the unconscious Caney. Then he swept a generous portion of free lunch into his hat and tossed it over the crowning woodwork of the ten-foot refrigerator, with the level motion of a mason tossing bricks to his mate. Caney's revolver followed, then Weir's and his own. He darted behind the bar and confiscated a half-filled bottle of wine, the appetizing name of which had won his approving notice earlier in the evening. He stepped on a chair beside the refrigerator, leaped up, caught the oaken edge of it, swung up with a supple twist of his strong young body, and dropped to the top of the refrigerator, safe hidden by the two-foot parapet of ornamental woodwork.

A little later two men sprang together through the front door; a sloe-eyed Mexican and the dwarfish friend of the Australian giant. They leaped aside to left and right, guns ready; they looked into the gambling hall; they flanked the bar, one at each end, and searched behind it.

Then the little man went to the door and

called out scornfully: "Come in, you damn cowards! He's gone!"

Shadowy forms grew out of the starlight, with whistlings, answered from afar; more shadows came.

"Is Caney dead?" inquired a voice.

"Hell, I don't know and I don't care!" answered the little man truculently. "I had no time to look at Caney, not knowing when that devil would hop me. See for yourself."

The crowd struggled in—but not all of them. Weir came in groaning, his face distorted with pain as he fondled his crippled arm. The Merman examined Caney. "Dead, nothing," he reported. "Knocked out. He won't breathe easy again for a week. Bring some whisky and a pail of water. Isn't this fine? I don't think! Billiard table ruined—plate-glass mirror shot to pieces—half a dozen men crippled, and that damned little hell hound got off scot-free!"

"You mention your men last, I notice," sneered the little man. "Art Price has got three of his back ribs caved in, and Lanning needs a full set of teeth—to say nothing of

He's Gone!

them run over by the stampede.   Jiminy, but you're a fine bunch!"

They poured water on Caney's head, and they poured whisky down Caney's throat; he gasped, spluttered, opened his eyes, and sat up, assisted by Hales and the Merman.

"Here—four of you chaps carry Caney to the doc," ordered the Merman.   "Take that door—break off the other hinge.   Tell doc a windlass got away from him and the handle struck him in the breast.   Tell him that he stopped the ore bucket from smashing the men at the bottom—sob stuff.   Coach Caney up, before you go in.   He's not so bad—he's coming to.   Fresh air will do him good, likely. Drag it, now."

"Say, Travis, I didn't see you doin' so much," muttered one of the gangsters as Caney was carried away, deathly sick.   He eyed the little man resentfully.   "Seems to me like you talk pretty big."

The little man turned on him in a fury.

"What the hell could I do?   Swept up in a bunch of blatting bull calves like that, and me the size I am?   By the jumping Jupiter, if I could have got the chance I would 'a' stayed for one fall if he had been the devil himself, pitchfork, horns and tail! As it was, I'm blame well thankful I wasn't stomped to death."

"All this proves what I was telling you," said Hales suavely. "If you chaps intend to stretch Johnny Dines, to-night's the only time. If one puncher can do this to you"—he surveyed the wrecked saloon with a malicious grin—"what do you expect when the John Cross warriors get here? It's now or never."

"Never, as far as I'm concerned," declared the bullet-headed man of the free lunch. "I'm outclassed. I've had e-nough! I'm done and I'm gone!"

"Never for me too. And I'm done with this pack of curs—done for all time," yelped the little man. "I'm beginning to get a faint idea of what I must look like to any man that's even half white. Little See is worth the whole boiling of us. For two cents I'd hunt him up and kiss his foot and be his Man Friday—if he'd have me. I begin to think Dines never killed Forbes at all. Forbes was shot in the back, and Shaky Akins says Dines is just such another as Charlie See. And Shaky would be a decent man himself if he didn't have to pack soapstones. I'll take his word for Dines. As sure as I'm a foot high, I've a good mind to go down to the jail and throw in with Gwinne."

"You wouldn't squeal, Travis?" pleaded the Merman. "You was in this as deep as the rest of us, and you passed your word."

"Yes, I suppose I did," agreed the little man reluctantly. Then he burst into a sudden fury. "Damn my word, if that was all! Old Gwinne wouldn't have me—he wouldn't touch me with a ten-foot pole. I've kept my word to scum like you till no decent man will believe me under oath." He threw up his hands with a tragic gesture. "Oh, I've played the fool!" he said. "I have been a common fool!"

He turned his back deliberately to that enraged crew of murderers and walked the length of the long hall to the back door. From his hiding place above the big refrigerator Charlie See raised his head to peer be-

tween the interstices and curlicues of the
woodwork so he might look after this later
prodigal.   Charlie was really quite touched,
and he warmed toward the prodigal all the
more because that evildoer had wasted no regret on wickedness, but had gone straight to
the root of the matter and reserved his remorse
for the more serious offense.   This was
Charlie's own view in the matter of fools; and
he was tolerant of all opinion which matched
his own.   But Charlie did not wear a sym-
pathetic look; he munched contentedly on a
cheese sandwich.

"Never mind Travis," said the Merman.
"Let him go.   The little fool won't peach, and
that's the main thing.   I'm going after Dines
now, if we did make a bad start.   There's
plenty of us here, and I can wake up two of my
dealers who will stand hitched.   And that
ain't all.   A bunch from the mines will drop
down for a snifter at eleven o'clock, when the
graveyard shift goes on and they come off.
I'll pick out those I can trust.   Some of 'em
are tough enough to suit even Travis—though

I doubt if they'd take any kinder to pool balls than you boys did—not till they got used to 'em. I don't blame you fellows. Billiard balls are something new."

"We want to get a move on, before the moon gets up," said Weir.

"Oh, that's all right! Lots of time. We'll stretch Mr. Dines, moonrise or not," said the Merman reassuringly. "But we'll meet the night shift at the bridge as they come off, and save a lot of time. Let's see now—Ames, Vet Blackman, Kroner, Shaw, Lithpin Tham—"

On the refrigerator, Charlie See put by his lunch. He fished out a tally book and pencil and began taking down names.

Charlie See raced to Perrault's door a little before eleven. He slipped in without a summons, he closed the door behind him and leaned his back against it. The waiting men rose to meet him—Perrault, Maginnis, Preisser, and a fourth, whom Charlie did not know.

"Come on to the jail, Maginnis! The gang

have closed up the Mermaid and they are now organizing their lynchin' bee. We've just time to beat 'em to it!"

"How many?" asked Perrault, reaching up for a rifle.

"You don't go, Perrault. This is no place for a family man."

"But, Spinal—"

"Shut up! No married man in this. Nor you, Preisser. You're too old. Mr. See, this is Buck Hamilton. Shall we get someone else? Shaky Akins? Where's Lull?"

"Lull is asleep. Let him be. Worn out. Akins is—we've no time for Akins. Here's a plenty—us three, the jailer and Dines. Jailer all right, is he?"

"Any turn in the road. Do you usually tote three guns, young feller?"

"Two of these are momentums—no, mementos," said Charlie. I've been spoiling the Egyptians. Spoiled some six or eight, I guess —and a couple more soured on the job. That'll keep. Tell you to-morrow. Let's go!"

"Vait! Vait!" said Preisser. "Go by my

place—I'll gome vith you so far—science shall
aid your brude force. Perrault and me, you
say, ve stay here. Ve are not vit to sed in der
vorevront of battles—vat? Good! Then ve
vill send to represend us my specimens. I haf
two lufly specimens of abblied psygology, gal-
gulated to haf gontrolling influence vith a mob
at the—ah, yes!—the zoölogical moment!
You vill see, you vill say I am quide righdt!
Gome on!"

"And they aim to get here sudden and
soon?" Mr. George Gwinne smiled on his
three visitors benevolently. That's good.
We won't have long to wait. I hate waiting. Bad for the nerves. Well, let's get a
wiggle. What you got in that box, Spinal?
Dynamite?"

Spinal grinned happily.

"Ho! Dynamite? My, you're the des-
prit character, ain't you? Dynamite? Not
much. Old stuff, and it shoots both ways.
We're up-to-date, we are. This here box, Mr.
Gwinne—we have in this box the last straw
that broke the camel's back. Listen!"

He held up the box. Gwinne listened. His smile broadened.   He sat down suddenly and—the story hates to tell this—Mr. Gwinne giggled.   It was an unseemly exhibition, particularly from a man so large as Mr. Gwinne.

"Going to give Dines a gun?" inquired Hamilton.

Mr. Gwinne wiped his eyes. "No. That wouldn't be sensible. They'd spring a light on us, see Dines, shoot Dines, and go home. But they don't want to lynch us and they'll hesitate about throwing the first shot. We'll keep Dines where he is."

He led the way to Johnny's cell.   The conversation had been low-voiced; Johnny was asleep.   Gwinne roused him.

"Hey, Johnny!   When is your friend coming to break you out?"

"Huh?" said Johnny.

"If he shows up, send him to the back door, and I'll let him in. We're going to have a lynchin' bee presently."

"Why, that was me!" said Charlie.

"Oh, was it?   Excuse me.   I didn't recognize your voice. You was speakin' pretty low, you see. I was right round the corner. Dog heard you, and I heard the dog. Well, that's too bad. We could use another good man, right now." Mr. Gwinne spoke the last words with some annoyance. "Well, come on —let's get everything ready. You fellows had better scatter round on top of the cells. I reckon the iron is thick enough to turn a bullet. Anyhow, they can't see you. I'll put out the light. I'm going to have a devil of a time to keep this dog quiet. I'll have to stay right with him or he'll bark and spoil the effect."

"They're coming," announced Spinal Maginnis, from a window. "Walkin' quiet—but I hear 'em crossin' the gravel."

"By-by, Dinesy," said See. "I've been rolling my warhoop, like you said."

The jail was dark and silent. About it shadows mingled, scattered, and gathered again. There was a whispered colloquy. Then a score of shadows detached themselves from the gloom. They ranged themselves in a line opposite the jail door. Other shadows crept from either side and took stations along the wall, ready to rush in when the door was broken down.

A low whistle sounded. The men facing the door came forward at a walk, at a trot, at a run. They carried a huge beam, which they used as a battering ram. As they neared the door the men by the jail wall crowded close. At the last step the beam bearers increased their pace and heaved forward together.

Unlocked, unbolted, not even latched, the door flung wide at the first touch, and whirled crashing back against the wall; the crew of the battering ram, braced for a shock, fell sprawling across the threshold. Reserves from the sides sprang over them, too eager to note the ominous ease of that door forcing, and plunged into the silent darkness of the jail.

They stiffened in their tracks. For a shaft of light swept across the dark, a trembling cone of radiance, a dancing light on the clump of masked men who shrank aside from that

The Lynchers

shining circle, on a doorway where maskers crowded in. A melancholy voice floated through the darkness.

"Come in," said Gwinne. "Come in—if you don't mind the smoke."

The lynchers crowded back, they huddled against the walls in the darkness beyond that cone of dazzling light.

"Are you all there?" said Gwinne. His voice was bored and listless. "Shaw, Ellis, Clark, Clancy, Tucker, Woodard, Bruno, Toad Hales—"

"I want Sim!" announced Charlie See's voice joyously. "Sim is mine. Somebody show me which is Sim! Is that him pushin' back toward the door?"

A clicking sound came with the words, answered by similar clickings here and there in the darkness.

"Tom Ross has got Sim covered," said the unhurried voice of Spinal Maginnis. "You and Hiram Yoast be sure to get that big fellow in front. I got my man picked."

A chuckle came from across the way. "You, Vet Blackman! Remember what I told you? This is me—Buck Hamilton. You're my meat!"

"Oh, keep still and let me call the roll," complained Gwinne's voice—which seemed to have shifted its position. "Kroner, Jody Weir, Eastman, Wiley, Hover, Lithpin Tham—"

The beam of light shifted till it lit on the floor halfway down the corridor; it fell on three boxes there.

From the outer box a cord led up through the quivering light. This cord tightened now, and raised a door at the end of the box; another cord tilted the box steeply.

"Look! Look! Look!" shrieked someone by the door.

Two rattlesnakes slid squirming from the box into that glowing circle—they writhed, coiled, swayed. *Z-z-z—B-z-z-zt!* The light went out with a snap.

"Will you fire first, gentlemen of the blackguards?" said Gwinne.

Someone screamed in the dark—and with that scream the mob broke. Crowding, cursing, yelling, trampling each other, fighting, the lynchers jammed through the door; they crashed through a fence, they tumbled over boulders—but they made time.   A desultory fusillade followed them; merely for encouragement.

XII

"Ostrich, *n.* A large bird to which (for its sins, doubtless) nature has denied the hinder toe in which so many pious naturalists have seen a conspicuous evidence of design. The absence of a good working pair of wings is no defect, for, as has been ingeniously pointed out, the ostrich does not fly."
—*The Devil's Dictionary.*

"Fare you well:
Hereafter, in a better world than this,
I shall desire more love and knowledge of you."
—*As You Like It.*

MR. BENJAMIN ATTLEBURY WADE paced a narrow beat on the matted floor. Johnny Dines, shirt-sleeved, in the prisoners' box, leaned forward in his chair to watch, delighted. Mr. Benjamin Attlebury Wade was prosecuting attorney, and the mat was within the inclosure of the court room, marked off by a wooden rail to separate the law's machinery from the materi— That has an unpleasant sound. To separate the taxpayer from— No, that won't do. To separate the performers from the spectators—that is much better. But even that has an offensive sound. Unintentionally so; groping, we near the heart of the mystery; the rail was to keep back the crowd and prevent confusion. That it has now become **a** sacramental barrier, a symbol and a sign of esoteric mystery, is not the rail's fault; it is the fault of the people on each side of the rail.

Mr. Wade had been all the long forenoon examining Caney and Weir, and was now searching the deeps of his mind for a last question to put to Mr. Hales, his last witness. Mr. Wade's brow was furrowed with thought; his hands were deep in his own pockets. Mr. Wade's walk was leisurely important and fascinating to behold. His foot raised slowly and very high, very much as though those pocketed hands had been the lifting agency. When he reached the highest point of each step his toe turned up, his foot paused, and then felt furtively for the floor—quite as if he were walking a rope, or as if the floor might not be there at all. The toe found the floor, the heel followed cautiously, they planted themselves on the floor and took a firm grip there; after which the other foot ventured forward. With such stealthy tread the wild beast of prey creeps quivering to pounce upon his victim. But Mr. Wade never leaped. And he was not wild.

The court viewed Mr. Wade's constitutional with some impatience, but Johnny Dines was charmed by it; he felt a real regret when Mr. Wade turned to him with a ferocious frown and snapped: "Take the witness!"

Mr. Wade parted his coat tails and sat down, performing that duty with the air of a sacrament. Johnny did not rise. He settled back comfortably in his chair and looked benevolently at the witness.

"Now, Mr. Hales, about that yearling I branded in Redgate cañon—what color was it?"

Mr. Wade rose, indignant.

"Your honor, I object! The question is irrelevant, incompetent and immaterial. Aside from its legal status, such a question is foolish and absurd, and an insult to the court."

"Why, now, I didn't object to any of your foolish and absurd questions all morning." Johnny's eyes widened with gentle reproach. "I let you ask all the questions you wanted."

Mr. Wade's nose twisted to a triumphant sneer.

" 'He who is his own lawyer has a fool for a client!' "

"I didn't want to take any unfair advantage," explained Johnny.

"Gentlemen! Gentlemen!" expostulated the court.

"You gallows meat!" snarled Wade. "You dirty—"

Johnny shook his head in a friendly warning. "He means you, too," he whispered.

The gavel fell heavily. The court rose up and the court's eyes narrowed.

"This bickering has got to stop! It is disgraceful. I don't want to see any more of it. Mr. Wade, for that last remark of yours you ought to pay a heavy fine, and you know it very well. This prisoner is being tried for murder. That does not make him a murderer. Your words were unmanly, sir."

"May it please the court," said Wade, white faced and trembling with rage, "I acknowledge myself entirely wrong, and I beg the court's pardon. I own that I was exasperated. The prisoner insulted me grossly."

"You insulted him first. You have been

doing it right along. You lawyers are always browbeating witnesses and prisoners. You get 'em where they can't talk back and then you pelt 'em with slurs and hints and sneers and insults. You take a mean advantage of your privileged position to be overbearing and arrogant. I've watched you at it. I don't think it is very sporting to say in the court room what you wouldn't dare say on the street. But when someone takes a whack at you— wow! that's different! Then you want the court to protect you." He paused to consider.

The justice of the peace—Judge Hinkle, Andy Hinkle—was a slim, wizened man, brown handed, brown faced, lean and wrinkled, with thin gray hair and a thin gray beard and faded blue eyes, which could blaze blue fire on occasion. Such fire, though a mild one, now died away from those old eyes, and into them crept a slightly puzzled expression. He looked hard at Mr. Wade and he looked hard at Mr. Dines. Then he proceeded.

"Mr. Wade, this court— Oh, let's cut out the court—that makes me tired! 'This court fines you twenty-five dollars for contempt of court.' How would that sound?"

Wade managed a smile, and bowed, not ungracefully. "It would sound unpleasant —perhaps a little severe, sir."

The court twinkled. "I was only meaning how silly it seemed to a plain man for him to have to refer to himself as the court. I'm not going to fine you, Mr. Wade—not this time. I could, of course, but I won't. It would be unfair to lecture you first and then fine you. Besides, there is something else. You have had great provocation and I feel compelled to take that into consideration. Your apology is accepted. I don't know who began it—but if you have been insulting the prisoner it is no less true that the prisoner has been aggravating you. I don't know as I ever saw a more provoking man. I been keepin' an eye on him —his eyebrows, the corners of his eyes, the corners of his mouth, his shoulder-shrugging, and his elbows, and his teeth and his toes. Mr. Wade, your moldy old saw about a fool for a client was never more misplaced. This man can out talk you and never open his mouth.   I'd leave him alone if I was you—he might make a fool of you."

Johnny half opened his mouth.   The judge regarded him sternly.   The mouth closed hastily.   Johnny dimpled.   The judge's hammer fell with a crash.

"I give you both fair notice right now," said Judge Hinkle, "if you start any more of this quarreling I'm goin' to slap on a fine that'll bring a blister."

Johnny rose timidly and addressed the court.

"Your Honor, I'm aimin' to 'tend strictly to my knittin' from now on.   But if I should make a slip, and you do have to fine me— couldn't you make it a jail sentence instead? I'm awful short of money, Your Honor."

He reached behind him and hitched up the tail of his vest with both hands, delicately; this accomplished, he sank into his chair, raised his trousers gently at the knee and gazed about him innocently.

"My Honor will be—"

The judge bit the sentence in two, leaving the end in doubt; he regarded the prisoner with baleful attention. The prisoner gazed through a window. The judge beckoned to Mr. Gwinne, who sat on the front seat between See and Hobby Lull. Mr. Gwinne came forward. The judge leaned across the desk.

"Mr. Gwinne, do you feed this prisoner well?"

"Yes, sir."

"About what, now, for instance?"

"Oh—beefsteak, ham and eggs, *enchilados,* canned stuff—most anything."

"Mr. Gwinne, if I told you to put this prisoner on a strict ration, would you obey orders?"

"I certainly would."

"That's all," said the judge. "Thank you. Mr. Dines, you may go on with the case. The witness may answer the question. Objection overruled. State your question again, Mr. Dines."

"Mr. Hales, will you tell His Honor what color was the calf I branded in Redgate Cañon, day before yesterday, about two o'clock in the afternoon?"

"I don't know," answered Hales sulkily.

"Oh! You didn't see it, then?"

"No."

"Then you are not able to state that it was a calf belonging to Adam Forbes?"

"No."

Johnny's eyes sought the window. "Nor whether it was a calf or a yearling?"

"Of course not."

"Did you see me brand the calf?"

"I did not!" Hales spat out the words with venomous emphasis. Johnny was unmoved.

"Will you tell the court if the brand I put on this heifer calf or bull yearling was my brand or Adam Forbes' brand?"

The gavel fell.

"Objection!" barked Wade.

"Sustained. The question is improperly put. The witness need not answer it. The counsel for the defense need not continue along these lines. I am quite able to distinguish between evidence and surmise, between a stated fact and unfair suggestion."

"Does Your Honor mean to insinuate—"

"Sit down, Mr. Wade! Sit down! My Honor does not mean to insinuate anything.

My Honor means to state that you have been trying to throw dust in my eyes. My Honor wishes to state that you should never have been allowed to present your evidence in any such shape, and if the prisoner had been represented by a competent lawyer you would not have been allowed—"

The judge checked himself; his face fell; he wheeled his chair slowly and glared at the prisoner with awful solemnity. "Dines! Is that why you made no objections? So the prosecuting attorney would queer himself with this court by attempting unfair tactics? Answer me, sir!"

"But is it likely, Your Honor, that I could see ahead as far as that?"

"Humph!" snorted His Honor. He turned back to the prosecuting attorney. "Mr. Wade, I am keeping cases on you. Your questions have been artfully framed to lead a simple old man astray—to bewilder him until he is ready to accept theory, surmise and suggestion as identical with a statement of facts or statements purporting to be facts. I'm simple and old, all right—but I never did learn to lead."

Mr. Benjamin Attlebury Wade sprang to his feet.

"Your Honor, I protest! You have been openly hostile to the prosecution from the first."

"Ah!" said the judge mildly. "You fear my remarks may unduly influence my decision—is that it? Calm yourself, Mr. Wade. I cannot say that I blame you much, however. You see, I think United States, and when I have to translate into the customary idiomcies of the law I do a bum job." He turned his head and spoke confidentially to the delighted court room. "Boys, it's gettin' me!" he said. "Did you hear that chatter I put out, when all I wanted to say was that I still knew sugar from salt and sawdust from cornmeal—also, in any case of extreme importance, as hereinbefore mentioned, and taking in consideration the fine and subtle nuisances of delicate thought, as it were, whereas, being then and there loaded with shot and slugs, I can still tell a hawk from a handsaw. Why, I'm getting so I talk that jargon to my jackass when I wallop him over the place made and provided on him, the said jackass, with a *curajo* pole! I'll tell you what —the first man I catch voting for me next year I'm going to pat him over the head with a pickhandle. You may proceed with the case, Mr. Dines."

"This is an outrage!" bawled the furious and red-faced prosecutor. "This is an outrage! An outrage! These proceedings are a mockery! This whole trial is a travesty on justice!"

The gavel banged down.

"This court is now adjourned," announced Judge Hinkle.

He leaned back in his chair and sighed luxuriously. He took out a pair of steel-rimmed spectacles and polished them; he held them poised delicately in one hand and beamed benevolently on the crowded court room.

"We have had a very trying forenoon," observed Mr. Hinkle blandly. "Perhaps some of us are ruffled a little. But I trust that nothing which has happened in this court room will cause any hard feeling of a lasting character. And I strongly advise that under no circumstances will any of you feel impelled to take any man and put his head under a pump, and pump on his head." The gavel rapped smartly. "This court will now come to order! Mr. Dines, as I remarked before recess, you will now proceed with the case."

"I'll not detain you long, Mr. Hales," said Johnny. "I didn't bother to cross-examine the previous witnesses"—he smiled upon Caney and Weir—"because they are suffering from the results of an accident. In the mines, as I hear. Mining is a dangerous business. Very. Sometimes a man is just one-sixteenth of a second slow—and it gets him trouble. I understand, Mr. Haies, that you three gentlemen were together when you found the murdered man?"

"Yes."

"You had been prospecting together?"

"Prospecting, and looking for saddle thieves."

"Did you find the saddle thieves?"

"No; I told you once."

"No," said Johnny; "you told Mr. Wade. Find any mines?"

"Yes."

"Good prospect?"

"I think so."

"Um—yes." Johnny hesitated, and fell silent. Hales fidgeted. "And the murdered man," began Johnny slowly, and stopped. Hales heaved a sigh of relief. Johnny darted a swift glance at the judge. "And the murdered man had been shot three times?"

"Three times. In the back."

"The shots were close together?"

"Yes. My hand would have covered all three."

"Sure of that?"

"Positive."

"In your opinion, these shots had been fired at close range?"

An interruption came. Four men trooped into the door, booted and spurred; three of the John Cross men—Tom Ross, Frank Bojarquez, Will Foster; with Hiram Yoast, of the Bar Cross: four fit to stand by Cæsar. A stir ran through the court room. They raised their hands to Johnny in grave salute; they filed to a bench together.

Johnny repeated the question: "You say, Mr. Hales, that these three shots had been fired at close range?"

"The dead man's shirt was burned. The gun must have been almost between his shoulder blades."

"Was there any blood on Forbes' saddle?"

"I didn't see Forbes' saddle," growled Hales; "or Forbes' horse."

"Oh, yes. But in your opinion, Forbes was riding when he was killed?"

"In my opinion, he was."

"What makes you think so?"

"We found the tracks where Forbes was dragged, twenty feet or so, before his foot come loose from the stirrup, and blood in the track all the way. I told all this before."

"So you did, so you did. Now about these wounds. Did the path of the bullets range up or down from where they entered the body?"

"Down."

"Sure of that?"

"Yes."

"Did you examine the body?"

"How else would I know? Of course I did."

"Show the court, on your own body, about where the wounds were located."

"They went in about here"—indicating—"and come out about here."

"Thank you. Then the shots passed obliquely through the body, entering behind, somewhere near the left shoulder blade, and coming out at a point slightly lower, and under the right breast?"

"About that, yes."

"All indicating that the murderer rode at his victim's left hand, and a little behind him, when these shots were fired?"

"I think so, yes."

"And that the gun muzzle must have been a little higher than the wounds made by the entering bullets, because the bullets passed through the body with a slightly downward trend?"

"That is right."

"How big was the murdered man?"

"He was a very large man."

"Very heavy or very tall?"

"Both, I should say.   It is hard to judge a dead man's height.   He was very heavily built."

"You lifted him?"

"I turned him over."

"How tall was he, would you say?"

"I tell you, I don't know."   Hales was visibly more impatient with each question.

"Of course you don't know.   But you can make a guess.   Come, give the court your estimate."

"Not less than six feet, I should say.   Probably more."

"Did you see Adam Forbes' horse—no, you told us that.   But you saw my horse when you arrested me?"

"Yes."

"Was my horse a small horse or a large one?"

"A small one."

Johnny rose and strolled to the window.

"Well, about how high?"

"About fourteen hands. Possibly an inch more."

"Would you know my horse again?"

"Certainly."

"So you could swear to him?"

"Yes."

"What color was he?"

"A *grullo*—a very peculiar shade of *grullo* —a sleek glossy, velvety blue."

"Was he thin or fat?"

"Neither. Smooth—not fat."

"Did you notice his brand?"

"Of course."

"Describe it to the court."

"He was branded K I M on the left hip."

"On which side did his mane hang?"

"On the left."

"Thank you. Now, Mr. Hales, would you describe me as a large man or a small one?"

Hales looked an appeal to the prosecutor.

"I object to that question—improper, irrelevant, incompetent and immaterial. And that is not all. This man, this man Dines, is arguing the case as he goes along, contrary to all rule."

"I like it that way," observed the judge placidly. "If he makes his point as the evidence is given, I'm not likely to miss any bets, as I might do if he waited for the summing up."

"I objected to the question," snapped the prosecutor. "I demand your ruling."

"Has the defense anything to offer? That question would certainly seem to be superfluous on the face of it," said the court, mildly.

"Your Honor," said Johnny, "I want to get this down on the record in black and white. Someone who has never seen me may have to pass on this evidence before we get done. I want that person to be sure of my size."

"Objection overruled."

"Please describe me—as to size—Mr. Hales."

"A very small man," answered Hales sulkily.

"In your opinion, when I shot Adam Forbes did I stand on my saddle? Or could I have inflicted a wound such as you have described by simply kneeling on my saddle—"

"I object!"

"—if Adam Forbes rode a horse big enough to carry his weight, and I rode a horse fourteen hands high?"

Wade leaped to his feet and flung out his hands. "I object!" he shrilled.

"Objection sustained. The question is most improper. I shall instruct myself to disregard it in making my decision."

"That's all," said Johnny Dines; and sat down.

"Any more witnesses for the prosecution, Mr. Wade?"

"No, sir. The prosecution rests."

The judge turned back to Johnny. "Witnesses for the defense?"

"Call my horse," said Johnny Dines.

"Your Honor, I object! This is preposterous—unheard of! We will admit the height of this accursed horse as being approximately fourteen hands, if that is what he wants to prove. I ask that you keep this buffoon in order. The trial has degenerated into farce-comedy."

"Do you know, Mr. Wade, I seem to observe some tragic elements in this trial," observed Hinkle. "I am curious to hear Mr. Dines state his motive in making so extraordinary a request from the court."

"He's trying to be funny!"

"No," said the judge; "I do not think Mr. Dines is trying to be funny. If such is his idea, I shall find means to make him regret it. Will you explain, Mr. Dines? You are entitled to make a statement of what you expect to prove."

Johnny rose.

"Certainly. Let me outline my plan of defense. I could not call witnesses until I heard the evidence against me. Now that I have heard the evidence, it becomes plain that, except for a flat denial by myself, no living man can speak for me. I was alone. When I take the stand presently, I shall state under oath precisely what I shall now outline to you briefly.

"On the day in question I was sent by Cole

Ralston to Hillsboro to execute his orders, as I will explain in full, later. I came through MacCleod's Park, started up a Bar Cross cow and her unbranded yearling, and I caught the yearling at the head of Redgate. While I was branding it, a big man—I have every reason to believe that this man was Adam Forbes—came down the cañon. He rode up where I was branding the yearling, talked to me, smoked a cigarette, gave me a letter to mail, and went back the way he came. I went to Garfield. My horse had lost a shoe, as the witnesses have stated. I nailed on a fresh shoe in Garfield, and came on. I was arrested about dark that night while on the road to Hillsboro. That is all my story. True or false, I shall not vary from it for any cross-examination.

"I shall ask Your Honor to consider that my story may be true. I shall ask Your Honor to consider that if my story is true no man may speak for me. I saw no other man between Upham and the Garfield ditch—twenty-five miles.

"You have heard the prosecution's theory.

It is that I was stealing a calf belonging to the
dead man—branding it; that he caught me in
the act, and that I foully murdered him.   If
I can prove the first part of that theory to be
entirely false; if I can demonstrate that even
if I killed Adam Forbes I certainly did not
kill him in the manner or for the motive set
forth by the theory of the prosecution—then
you may perhaps believe my unsupported
statement as to the rest of it.   And that is what
I can do, if allowed the opportunity.   I cannot, by myself, now or at any other time, absolutely prove my statement to be true.   I can
and will prove the theory of the prosecution
to be absolutely false.   To do that I rely upon
myself—not upon my statement, but upon myself, my body, so much flesh and blood and
bone, considered as an exhibit in this case,
taken in connection with all known or alleged
facts; on myself and my horse; on Adam
Forbes' dead body and on the horse Adam
Forbes rode that day; on the Bar Cross yearling I branded day before yesterday, a yearling
that I can describe in detail, a yearling that
can be found and must be found, a yearling

that will be found following a Bar Cross cow.
I have no fancy to be hanged by a theory.   I
demand to test that theory by facts.   I demand
that my horse be called to testify to the facts."

"Mr. Gwinne, you may call the prisoner's
horse," said the justice.   "Spinal, you may act
as the court's officer while Gwinne is gone."

"His name is Twilight," added Johnny,
"and he is over at the Gans stables."

"I protest!   Your Honor, I protest against
such unmitigated folly," stormed Mr. Benjamin Attlebury Wade, in a hot fury of exasperation.   "You are making a mockery of
the law!   There is no precedent on record for
anything like this."

"Here's where we make a new precedent,
then," observed the court cheerfully.   "I have
given my instructions, and I'd be willing to
place a small bet on going through with my
folly.   I don't know much about the law, but
the people who put me here knew I didn't
know much about the law when they elected
me—so I guess they aimed to have me get at
the rights of things in my own way."   He
twisted his scanty beard for a moment; his

faded blue eyes peered over the rims of his glasses. "Not that it would make any great difference," he added.

A little wearied from the strain of focalized effort, Johnny looked out across the blur of faces. Hobby Lull smiled at him, and Charlie See looked hardihood like his own. There were other friendly faces, many of them; and beyond and above them all shone the faces of his straining mates, Hiram and the three John Cross men.

"Judge, may I speak to the prisoner?" asked Hiram Yoast. He tugged at a grizzled foretop.

"You may."

"Old-timer," said Hiram, "we didn't hear of you till late last night. We had moved on from Hermosa. That's all, Your Honor. Thank you."

"Will the learned counsel for the defense outline the rest of his program?" inquired the judge, with respectful gentleness.

"He will," said Johnny. "I'll have to ask you to continue the case until to-morrow, or maybe later—till I can get some of the Garfield men who can swear to the size of the horse Adam Forbes rode.   Then I want—"

Charlie See rose.

"I offer my evidence.   I slept with Adam Forbes the night before he was killed; and I saw him start.   He rode a big horse."

"Thank you," said Johnny.   "I'll call you after a while.   Get yourself a reserved seat inside here.   I knew Adam Forbes rode a big horse, and I can describe that horse—if Adam Forbes was the man I met in Redgate, which I've never doubted.   A big blaze-faced bay with a Heart-Diamond brand.   This way." He traced on the wall a heart with an inscribed diamond.   "But I want to call the men who brought in Adam Forbes.   I want to question them about all the tracks they saw, before it rained.   So you see, Your Honor, I'll have to ask for a continuation.   I can't afford to be hanged to save the county a little money."

"You'll get your continuation."

"But that isn't all.   That yearling I branded—he was from the river *bosques,* for he had his tail full of sand burs, and the bunch he was with was sure snaky.   His mammy's

a Bar Cross cow and he's a Bar Cross bull—
and so branded by me. He'll be back with
her by this time. He had all the Hereford
markings, just about perfect. His mammy
wasn't marked so good. She had a bald face
and a line back, all right, and white feet and
a white belly. But one of her stockings was
outsize—run clear up her thigh—and she had
two big white spots on her ribs on the nigh
side. I didn't see the other side. And one of
her horns drooped a little—the right one. I
would like to have you appoint a commission
to bring them into court, or at any rate to
interview them and get a statement of facts."

"That's reasonable," said the judge. "Ap-
plication granted." He called to Tom Ross.
"Tom, that's your job. You and your three
peelers find that Bar Cross cow—objection
overruled—and that bull yearling. Mr.
Clerk, you may so enter it, at the charge of
Sierra County."

Wade was on his feet again.

"But, Your Honor," he gasped, "those men
are the prisoner's especial friends!"

"Exactly. That's why they'll find that calf.

Results are what I'm after, and I don't care a hang about methods." He frowned. "Look here, Mr. Wade—am I to understand that you want this prisoner convicted whether he's guilty or not?"

"No, no, certainly not. But why appoint those four men in particular? There is always the possibility of collusion."

Judge Hinkle's face became bleak and gray. He rose slowly. The court room grew suddenly still. Hinkle walked across the little intervening space and faced the prosecutor.

"Collision, perhaps you mean," he said. His quiet, even voice was cutting in its contempt. "What do you think this is—a town full of thugs? I want you to know that those four men stand a damn sight higher in this community than you do. Sit down—you're making an indecent exposure of your soul!"

As he went back to his desk, an oldish man came to the door and caught Hobby Lull's eye. He beckoned. Hobby rose and went to the door. They held a whispered council in the anteroom.

Judge Hinkle busied himself with the

papers on his desk for a moment. When he looked up his face had regained its wonted color.

"Here comes Gwinne with the horse," announced Hobby Lull from the anteroom.

"Mr. Dines, how does your client propose to question that horse, if I may ask?" inquired the judge.

"I propose to prove by my horse," said Johnny, "that though I may have murdered this man I certainly did not shoot him while I was riding this horse. And I depend on the evidence of the prosecution's witnesses"—he smiled at the prosecution's witnesses—"to establish that no one rode in Redgate that day except me—and them! If the court will appoint some man known to be a rider and a marksman, and will instruct him to ride my horse by the courthouse windows, we can get this testimony over at once. It has been shown here that I carried a .45. Set up a box out there where we can see from the windows; give your man a gun and tell him to ride as close as he likes and put three shots in that box. If he hits that box more than once—"

"Gun-shy?" said Judge Hinkle.

"Watch him!" said Johnny rapturously.

The judge's eye rested on Mr. Wade with frank distaste.

"We will now have another gross instance of collusion," he announced. "I will call on Frank Bojarquez to assist the court."

Francisco Bojarquez upreared his straight length at the back of the hall.

"Excuse, please, if I seem to tell the judge what he is to do. But what Mistair Wade says, it is true a little—or it might seem true to estrangers. For us in Hillsboro, frien's togethair, eet does not mattair; we know. But because the worl' ees full of estrangers— theenk, Judge Hinkle, eef it is not bes' that it ees not a great frien' of the preesoner who is to examine that horse—what? That no estranger may have some doubts? There are so many estrangers."

"Humph! There is something in that." The justice scratched his ear. "Very well. George Scarboro, stand up. Are you acquainted with this prisoner?"

"No, sir."

"You are one of the Arizona Rangers?"

"I am."

"Slip your saddle on that blue horse.   You know what you have to do?"

"Yes, sir."

Scarboro departed, and half the court room went with him.   Five minutes later he rode the Twilight horse, prancing daintily, under the courthouse windows.   The windows were lined with faces.   Johnny, the judge and Wade had a window to themselves, within the sacred railing.   But Spinal Maginnis did not look from any window.   Spinal was looking elsewhere—at Caney, Weir and Hales.

The ranger wore a loose and sagging belt; his gun swung low on his thigh, just at the reach of his extended arm.   As he came abreast of the destined box Scarboro's arm flashed down and up.   So did Twilight.

A pistol shot, a long blue streak, and a squeal of anguish ascended together, hopelessly mingled and indiscriminate, spurning the spinning earth.   It launched toward outer space in a complex of motion upward, side-wise, forward and inside out, shaming the

orbit of the moon, nodes, perturbations,
apsides, syzygies and other symptoms too
luminous to mention; but perhaps apogee and
acceleration were the most prominent. A
clatter, a pitch, an agonized bawl, a sailing
hat, a dust cloud, a desperate face above it,
with streaming hair; the marvel fell away
down the hill and left a stunned silence behind. And presently a gun came down.

"Do you want to cross-examine the witness?" inquired Johnny.

Wade threw up his hands.

"Well!" he said. "Well!" His jaw
dropped. He drew Johnny aside and whispered, "See here, damn you—did you kill that
man?"

"No, I didn't," whispered Johnny. "But
you keep it dark. It's a dead secret."

The roaring crowd came in with laughter
and shouts. As they found seats and the
tumult quieted Johnny addressed the judge.

"Shall I take the stand now, Your Honor,
or wait till after dinner? It's late, I know—
but you'd believe me better right now—"

"Wait a minute, Andy!"

A man rose in the crowd—a tall old man with a melancholy face—the same who had summoned Hobby Lull to the door.

"Why, hello, Pete! I didn't see you come!" said the judge.

"That's funny, too. I have been here half an hour. You're getting old, Andy—getting old!"

"Oh, you go to thunder! Say, can you straighten up this mess?"

"I can help, at least—or so I believe. I was with the search party."

"Well, who calls this witness—the defense or the prosecution?" inquired the court.

"Oh, let me call myself—as the friend of the court, *amicus curiæ,* just as they used to do in England—do yet, for all I know. I've not heard your evidence—though I saw some just now, outside. But I've got a few facts which you may be able to fit in somewhere. I don't know the defendant, and am not for or against the prosecutor or for anybody or anything except justice. So I'll take it kindly if you'd let me tell my story in my own way—as the friend of justice. I'll get over the ground quicker and tell it straighter. If anyone is not satisfied they can cross-examine me afterwards, just as if I had been called by one side or the other."

Judge Hinkle turned to Wade. "Any objections?"

"No," said Wade. "I guess justice is what we all want—results, as you said yourself."

He was a subdued man. His three witnesses stirred uneasily, with sidelong glances. Spinal Maginnis kept a corner of his eye on those witnesses.

"Suits me," said Johnny.

"I got to get me a drink," whispered Caney, and rose, tiptoeing. But Maginnis rose with him.

"Sit down, Mr. Caney," he said. "You look poorly. I'll fetch you some water."

Pete Harkey took the stand and was duly sworn. He crossed his legs and addressed the judge.

"Well, we went up in Redgate, Dan Fenderson and I and a bunch. We thought there was no use of more than one coming here to-day, because we all saw just the same things."

Hinkle nodded. "All right, Pete. Tell us about it."

"Well, now, Andy—Your Honor—if it's just the same to everybody, I'll skip the part about the tracks and finding Adam until cross-examination. It's just going over the same old ground again. I've been talking to Hobby, and we found everything just about as you heard it from these boys." His eye shifted toward the witness bench. "All except one little thing about the tracks, and that was done after the murder, and might have been happen-so. And I was wanting to hurry up and get back to Garfield to-night. We're going to bury Adam at sundown."

"All right, Pete. But we'll cross-examine you—if not to-day, then to-morrow. It pays to work tailings, sometimes."

"That's queer, too. I was just coming to that—in a way. Mining. Adam went up there to prospect for gold—placer gold. When the big rain came, the night he was killed, all tracks were washed out, of course. We hadn't got far when dark came—and then the rain. But yesterday I went combing out the country to look for Adam's outfit of camp stuff, and also to see if perhaps he had found any claims before he was killed. And I found this."

He handed to the judge a small paper packet, folded and refolded, and wrapped round with a buckskin string. The judge opened it.

"Coarse gold!" he said. "Like the Apache gold in the seventies! Pete, you've got a rich mine if there's much of this."

"It is rich dirt," said Pete. "I got that from less than a dozen pans. But it is not my mine."

"How so?"

"I got home late last night. This morning I looked in all the pockets in the clothes Adam was wearing. Here is what I found in his vest." He handed to Hinkle a small tobacco sack, rolled to a tiny cylinder.

"The same kind of gold—big as rice!" said Hinkle. "So Adam Forbes found this?"

Caney's hand crept under his coat.

"Judge for yourself. I found three claims located. Three. But no name of Adam

Forbes to any notice.   One claim was called the 'Goblin Gold—' "

Charlie See rose up as if he were lifted by the hair of his head.   "The other names, Pete! Not the locators.   The claims—give me the names of the other two claims!"

" 'Nine Bucks' was one—and the 'Please Hush.' "

Charlie turned and took one step, his tensed weight resting on the balls of his feet, his left arm lashed out to point.   All eyes turned to the witness bench—and two witnesses looked at one.

"Caney!" thundered Charlie See.

Leaping, Caney's arm came from his coat. See's hand was swifter, unseen.   In flashes of fire and smoke, Caney, even as he leaped up, pitched forward on his face.   His arm reached out on the floor, holding a smoking gun, and See's foot was on the gun.

A dozen men had pulled down Toad Hales and Jody Weir.   Gwinne's gun was out.

"Stand back!   The next man over the rails gets it!"   Maginnis jumped beside him.   The shouting crowd recoiled.

"Sit down! Sit down, everybody!" shouted the judge. He pounded on his desk. "Bojarquez! Ross! Foster! Come up here. I make you deputies. Get this crowd out or get order."

The deafening turmoil stopped as suddenly as it had begun.

"Gwinne, arrest those two men for the murder of Adam Forbes," ordered Hinkle.

"Well, gee-whiz, I'd say they was under arrest now. Here, gimme them." He reached down and handcuffed Weir and Hales together. "How's Caney, Dines? Dead?"

Johnny knelt by the fallen man. "Dead as a door nail. Three shots. Did he get you anywhere, See?"

"No. He was just one-sixteenth of a second too late." Charlie See looked hard at the cylinder of his gun. He had fired only two shots. "Pete, it's a wonder he didn't hit you. You was right in line."

"I wasn't there," said Pete dryly. "Not when the bullets got there. Not good enough."

Gwinne and Maginnis took the two prisoners to jail, by the back door.

"Now for a clearing up," said Judge Hinkle. "You seem to have inside information, Mr. See. Suppose you tell us about it?"

"No chance for a mistake, judge. I had a long talk with Adam the night before, about a lost gold mine at Mescalero. And three of the phrases that we used back and forth—it seems he picked them out to name his find. 'Goblin Gold.' I used the word 'gobbling' gold—joking, you know. And the story was about 'nine bucks'; and it wound up with an old Mescalero saying 'Won't you please hush?' It wasn't possible that those three names had reached the papers Pete found, except through the dead man's mind. Adam called these three men to witness for him, likely. Then they killed him for his mines. They destroyed his location papers, but they kept the names. Easier than to make up new ones. That'll hang 'em."

"Sounds good. But how are you going to prove it? Suppose they get a good lawyer

and stick to their story?   They found a mine,
and you got in a shooting match with Caney.
That don't prove anything."

"Well, I'll bet I can prove it," said Johnny
Dines.   "Ten to one, that letter Forbes gave
me to mail was his location papers. He
seemed keen about it."

"Did he say anything about location papers?
Was the letter addressed to the recorder?"
demanded Pete.

"Look now!" said Johnny.   "If this theory
of See's is correct, and if that really was location papers in the letter I mailed—why, that
letter won't get here till two o'clock this afternoon, whether it is the location papers or what.
And the postmaster and the recorder are both
here in this court room, judge.   Gwinne was
pointing out everybody to me, before you
called court.   So they can mosey along down
to the post office together—the postmaster and
the recorder.   And when that letter comes
you'll know all about it."

"Ah, that reminds me," said the judge—
"the case of the Territory of New Mexico vs.

John Dines is now dismissed. This court is now adjourned. John Dines, I want to be the first to congratulate you."

"Thanks, Judge. —Hiram," said Johnny, "Cole told me to report to you. He said I was to go to the John Cross pasture and pick me a mount from the runaways there."

"But, Johnny, you can't ride those horses," said Bojarquez.

Johnny flushed. "Don't you believe it, old hand. You're not the only one that can ride."

Bojarquez spread out his hands. "But bareback? Where ees your saddle? And the Twilight horse? The bridle, he ees broke. Scarb'ro's in Chihuahua by now."

"Dinner's on me," said Johnny.

Charlie See drew Johnny aside and spoke to him in confidence.

"How does it happen you know so pat just when a letter gets to Hillsboro when it is posted in Garfield?"

"A letter? Oh—Hobby Lull, he told me."

"Yes, yes. And what was the big idea for keeping still about that letter while they wove a rope to your neck?"

"Why, my dear man," said Johnny, "I can't read through a sealed envelope."

Charlie sniffed. "You saw a good many things mighty clear, I notice, but you overlooked the one big bet—like fun you did! Caney and Weir and Hales—don't you suppose they knew that letter was on the way? And that it was never to reach the recorder?"

"Since you are so very shrewd," said Johnny, "I sometimes wonder that you are not shrewder still."

"And keep my mouth shut? That's how I shall keep it. But I just wanted you to know. You may be deceiving me, but you're not fooling me any. Keep your secret."

"Thank you," said Johnny, "I will."

"Good boy. All the same, Hobby and I will be up at the post office. And I know now what we'll find in that letter you mailed. We'll find Adam's location papers, with them three murderers for witness."

And they did. They found something else too; a message from beyond the grave that in his hour of fortune their friend did not forget his friends.

They buried Adam Forbes at sundown of that day. No thing was lacking; his friends and neighbors gathered together to bid him Godspeed; there were love and tears for him. And of those friends, three were all road stained and weary; they had ridden hard from Hillsboro for that parting; Lull and Charlie See and old Pete. It was to one of these that all eyes were turned when the rude coffin was lowered into the grave.

"Pete?" said Jim-Ike-Jones.

And old Pete Harkey stepped forth and spoke slowly, while his faded old eyes looked past the open grave and rested on the hills beyond.

"More than at any other time we strive to center and steady our thoughts, when we stand by the loved and dead. It is an effort as vain as to look full and steadily at the blinding sun. I can tell you no thing here which you do not know.

"You all knew Adam Forbes. He was a simple and kindly man. He brought a good courage to living, he was all help and laughter, he joyed in the sting and relish of rushing life.

Those of you here who were most unfriends to him will not soon forget that gay, reckless, tender-hearted creature.

"You know his faults. He was given to hasty wrath, to stubbornness and violence. His hand was heavy. If there are any here who have been wronged by this dead man—as I think most like—let the memory of it be buried in this grave. It was never his way to walk blameless. He did many things amiss; he took wrong turnings. But he was never too proud to turn back, to admit a mistake or to right his wrongdoing. He paid for what he broke.

"For the rest—he fed the hungry, helped the weak, he nursed the sick and dug graves for the dead. Now, in his turn, it is fitting and just that no bought hand dug this grave, but that his friends and his foes did him this last service, and called pleasant dreams to his long sleep.

"We have our dear dreams, too. It can do no harm to dream that somewhere down the skies that brightness and fire and light still flames—but not for us.

"It is written that upon Mars Hill the men of Athens built an altar 'to the Unknown God.' It was well builded; and with no misgiving we leave our friend to the care—and to the honor—of the Unknown God."

He stood back; and from the women who wept came one who did not weep, dry-eyed and pale; whose pitying hand dropped the first earth into the grave.

"Stardust to stardust," said Edith Harkey.

That night Pete Harkey stood by the big fireplace of the big lonesome house.

"Shall I light the fire, Edith?"

"Not to-night, father."

In the dimness he groped for a chair; he took her on his knee, her arms clung fast.

"Is it well with you, Edith?"

Then, in the clinging dusk she dared the truth at last; to ears that did not hear. For his thought was with the dead man. She knew it well; yet once to tell her story—only once! Her voice rang steady, prouder than any pride: "I have loved Greatheart. It is well with me."

"Poor little girl," he said. "Poor little girl!" The proud head sought his breast and now her tears fell fast.

And far away, Charlie See rode south through the wizard twilight. There was no singing now. For at the world's edge some must fare alone; through all their dreams one unforgotten face—laughing, and dear, and lost.

THE END

THE WESTERN FRONTIER LIBRARY, of which *Stepsons of Light* is Number 43, was started in 1953 by the University of Oklahoma Press. It is designed to introduce today's readers to the exciting events of our frontier past and to some of the memorable writings about them. The following list is complete as of the date of publication of this volume:

1. Prof. Thomas J. Dimsdale. *The Vigilantes of Montana*. With an introduction by E. DeGolyer.
2. A. S. Mercer. *The Banditti of the Plains*. With a foreword by William H. Kittrell.
3. Pat F. Garrett. *The Authentic Life of Billy, the Kid*. With an introduction by Jeff C. Dykes.
4. Yellow Bird (John Rollin Ridge). *The Life and Adventures of Joaquín Murieta*. With an introduction by Joseph Henry Jackson.
5. Lewis H. Garrard. *Wah-to-yah and the Taos Trail*. With an introduction by A. B. Guthrie, Jr.
6. Charles L. Martin. *A Sketch of Sam Bass, the Bandit*. With an introduction by Ramon F. Adams.
7. Washington Irving. *A Tour on the Prairies*. With an introduction by John Francis McDermott.
8. *X. Beidler: Vigilante*. Edited by Helen Fitzgerald Sanders in collaboration with William H. Bertsche, Jr. With a foreword by A. B. Guthrie, Jr.
9. Nelson Lee. *Three Years Among the Comanches*. With an introduction by Walter Prescott Webb.
10. *The Great Diamond Hoax and Other Stirring Incidents in the Life of Asbury Harpending*. With a foreword by Glen Dawson.
11. *Hands Up; or, Twenty Years of Detective Life in the Mountains and on the Plains*: Reminiscences by Gen-

319

eral D. J. Cook, Superintendent of the Rocky Mountain Detective Association. With an introduction by Everett L. DeGolyer, Jr.

12. Will Hale. *Twenty-Four Years a Cowboy and Ranchman in Southern Texas and Old Mexico*. With an introduction by A. M. Gibson.

13. Gen. John S. Brisbin, U.S.A. *The Beef Bonanza; or, How to Get Rich on the Plains*. With a foreword by Gilbert C. Fite.

14. Isabella L. Bird. *A Lady's Life in the Rocky Mountains*. With an introduction by Daniel J. Boorstin.

15. W. T. Hamilton, *My Sixty Years on the Plains*. With an introduction by Donald J. Berthrong.

16. *The Life of John Wesley Hardin, As Written by Himself*. With an introduction by Robert G. McCubbin.

17. Elizabeth Bacon Custer. *"Boots and Saddles"; or, Life in Dakota with General Custer*. With an introduction by Jane R. Stewart.

18. John F. Finerty. *War-Path and Bivouac; or, the Conquest of the Sioux*. With an introduction by Oliver Knight.

19. Frederic Remington. *Pony Tracks*. With an introduction by J. Frank Dobie.

20. Thomas Edgar Crawford. *The West of the Texas Kid*. Edited and with an introduction by Jeff C. Dykes.

21. Frank Collinson. *Life in the Saddle*. Edited and arranged by Mary Whatley Clarke. With drawings by Harold D. Bugbee.

22. *Fifty Years on the Trail: A True Story of Western Life*. The adventures of John Young Nelson as described to Harrington O'Reilly.

23. Edward Bonney. *The Banditti of the Prairies: A Tale of the Mississippi Valley*. With an introduction by Philip D. Jordan.

24. Walter Baron von Richthofen. *Cattle-raising on the Plains of North America*. With an introduction by Edward Everett Dale.

25. Captain Charles King, U.S.A. *Campaigning with Crook*. With an introduction by Don Russell.

26. *Life of Tom Horn, Government Scout and Interpreter, Written by Himself: A Vindication*. With an introduction by Dean Krakel.

27. Edward Everett Dale. *Cow Country*.

28. Elinor D. Gregg. *The Indians and the Nurse*.

29. E. E. White. *Experiences of a Special Indian Agent*. With an introduction by Edward Everett Dale.

30. *Frontier Trails: The Autobiography of Frank M. Canton*. Edited by Edward Everett Dale.

31. George Bird Grinnell. *When Buffalo Ran*.

32. O. C. Fisher, with J. C. Dykes. *King Fisher: His Life and Times*.

33. Elizabeth B. Custer. *Following the Guidon*. With an introduction by Jane R. Stewart.

34. J. Evetts Haley. *The XIT Ranch of Texas and the Early Days of the Llano Estacado*.

35. Herman W. Albert. *Odyssey of a Desert Prospector*.

36. Thomas C. Battey. *The Life and Adventures of a Quaker Among the Indians*. With an introduction by Alice Marriott.

37. Baylis John Fletcher. *Up the Trail in '79*. Edited and with an introduction by Wayne Gard.